THE
apo™
SERIES

VIGILANCE

6.99

The man took a few steps into the exhibit hall and paused as if daring the security cameras to pick him up. In fact, he appeared to be seeking out each of the video cameras to make sure they got a good shot.

Sydney sat up straighter as she waited for him to make his approach. She glanced back to Vaughn and noticed his fist sliding in the direction of his holstered gun. It was clear he wanted payback for the sneak attack on the ship. But Sydney knew he wouldn't do anything to jeopardize the fact-finding mission, and certainly nothing that would put the innocents in the room at risk.

The mystery man surveyed the room, his eyes stopping briefly on Vaughn before continuing. It was unlikely that he'd made Nadia or Marshall, or Weiss out in the hallway, but she assumed the man figured she and Vaughn were not alone. Sydney slid to the side of the bench, allowing room for the man. After a moment he walked over to her and took the space offered.

"Ms. Bristow," he said warmly as he sat. "Good to see you again."

Sydney was well practiced at keeping her facial features locked to hide her emotions. But she knew her eyes gave away the surprise at being so easily identified.

Also available from
SIMON SPOTLIGHT ENTERTAINMENT

THE
SERIES

TWO OF A KIND?

FAINA

COLLATERAL DAMAGE

REPLACED

THE ROAD NOT TAKEN

ALIAS™

THE apo™ SERIES

VIGILANCE

BY PAUL RUDITIS

An original novel based on the
hit TV series created by J. J. Abrams

SIMON SPOTLIGHT ENTERTAINMENT

New York   London   Toronto   Sydney

This book is a work of fiction. Any references to historical events, real people, or real locales are used fictitiously. Other names, characters, places, and incidents are the product of the author's imagination, and any resemblance to actual events or locales or persons, living or dead, is entirely coincidental.

SSE

SIMON SPOTLIGHT ENTERTAINMENT
An imprint of Simon & Schuster
1230 Avenue of the Americas, New York, New York 10020.
Text and cover art copyright © 2006 by Touchstone Television
All rights reserved, including the right of reproduction in whole or in part in any form.
SIMON SPOTLIGHT ENTERTAINMENT and related logo are trademarks of Simon & Schuster, Inc.
Manufactured in the United States of America
First Edition 10 9 8 7 6 5 4 3 2 1
Library of Congress Control Number 2005925955
ISBN-13: 978-1-4169-0928-6
ISBN-10: 1-4169-0928-1

FOR CHRISTINA

CHAPTER 1

BERN, SWITZERLAND

Sydney Bristow was so focused on the street around her that she barely noticed she was shivering from the cold. The chill winds blowing down from the Alps were an abrupt departure from the Los Angeles version of winter. Even a weekend trip to Big Bear wouldn't have prepared her for the record-low temperatures the city of Bern was currently experiencing. Though she could mentally ignore the cold, her body couldn't help but react.

Aside from the occasional car passing by, the street was not very busy. Even the Swiss knew when it was time to stay indoors. And they lived for this kind of weather. Sydney could hear sirens off in the distance, so it wasn't like the city was abandoned. It only *seemed* that way.

She wasn't entirely alone, though. A trio of bundled-up people were a short distance away. Tourists. Probably decided to save some money and see the sights during the off-season. They weren't about to let a stretch of subfreezing temperatures stop them. Two members of the trio were happily posing in front of the Kindlifresserbrunnen while the third took their picture. Then they exchanged places for different poses with each of their cameras. Sydney figured they'd get a kick out of showing the fountain to their friends back home. The appropriately named "Ogre Fountain" was an odd attraction, to say the least.

The sixteenth-century fountain itself was fairly basic: an octagonal pool at the base, empty during the winter season. It sat on the side of the road rather unceremoniously. Four spigots stretched out of the fountain's central tower. It was the statue sitting atop the tower that gave the fountain its name and sent an extra chill down Sydney's spine.

A plaster ogre held a bag full of struggling

children figures frozen in time. Even worse, one of the small children was gripped in the ogre's mouth, and the others watched in terror. Sydney had seen many things during her time as an agent for and (unknowingly) against the U.S. government, but this morbid tourist attraction was by far one of the strangest.

Sydney tore her eyes away from the odd fountain, silently scolding herself for letting her attention drift even for the brief moment. Ahead, a small red trolley had come and gone while she'd been staring at the fountain, but no one had gotten off, so she hadn't missed anything, really. Still, it was unlike her to let her mind wander during a mission.

It wasn't as if she were expecting anything exciting to happen. Her life wasn't in any more peril than it was on the average day. It was just a simple meet. But it was still nice to know she had a guardian watching over her.

"Have I mentioned how much I hate this?" Sydney said softly into the cold air. The communicator hidden inside a pin stuck on her black leather coat picked up her words and transmitted them into the gray stone building beside her. It wasn't a great place to observe the meet, but their options had been limited by the layout of the street and the fact that Sydney hadn't been the one to pick the location. If she had, she would have been waiting indoors now, preferably by a fire.

"It shouldn't be much longer," Michael Vaughn's voice replied in her earpiece. "Then we'll get some hot chocolate and warm you up."

"That's not what I meant," she said.

"I know," Vaughn said. "But hot chocolate works for anything that ails you."

Sydney raised her chin and directed a smile up at him. She knew he could see it clearly through the binoculars from his position in the third-story window. Even though he was inside, she knew that he also wasn't totally embraced in warmth. He had to keep the window open for a clean shot if it became necessary.

She brushed aside a strand of synthetic blond hair and checked her watch. The contact was ten minutes late. Not that punctuality would have endeared him to her in any way. It was just that any divergence from a prearranged plan put her senses on heightened alert.

Sydney maintained her continuous scan of the street. The tourists were already putting away their digital cameras and shuffling toward the warmth of a small restaurant on the first floor of the building in which Vaughn was stationed. *Looks like they finally gave in and accepted the fact that they can't win against the weather*, Sydney thought.

She couldn't blame them. If she'd had her choice, she'd be right behind them. Actually, if it were up to her, she'd be at home right now enjoying the view of the Alps while sitting on the couch in her pajamas and watching *The Sound of Music*.

She was only alone on the street for a minute when she saw a man coming around the corner at the north end of the street. She had expected her contact to pull up in a car, so her attention wasn't focused on him at first. *Who would be out for a stroll on a day like this?* she wondered.

He could have been just a local heading home for the evening, but the two men flanking him one step behind screamed *bodyguards*. It annoyed Sydney that he wasn't even bothering to look inconspicuous.

Sydney turned her full attention to the trio of men walking toward her. Vaughn had the street covered, so she would be warned if anyone came up behind her. She locked eyes with the contact. He had made it clear that there was no need for secret phrases or furtive tells. *I always conduct my business in the open,* he had written over the secured communications system he had set up for his business. *It's more honest that way.*

Sydney still couldn't get over the total lack of irony in his statement.

One of the guards peeled off about thirty feet away from her and took up a position with his back to the building Vaughn was stationed inside. The other guard continued forward, passing Sydney without bothering to acknowledge her. He took up a position twenty feet behind her, standing in the exact same manner as his friend. She didn't like that he was behind her, but she knew Vaughn would have his eyes trained on the man.

"I believe you've been waiting for me," her contact said as he approached.

"Yes," Sydney said. In the long list of crimes against him, she couldn't understand why his not apologizing for his lateness was the thing that really upset her.

"Maximilian Sprague," he said, holding out his hand.

Sydney took his hand. "Lilia Von Malkin. It is a pleasure to meet you, Mr. Sprague."

"Please call me Maxie," he said as his hand lingered in hers long past what would be considered proper. Or comfortable.

"I don't believe I will," Sydney said as she forced his hand away. "Mr. Sprague."

"A feisty one, aren't you, Lilia?"

There was something particularly annoying about the combination of congenial and condescending. Sydney just added it to the list and moved on. It wouldn't help the situation any for her to come across as overly aggressive. She had a role to play, and she would cope by immersing herself in the part.

"Are you sure you wouldn't rather move to someplace less exposed?" Sydney asked as she looked down the still-empty street. The rows of trees across the road concerned her, but not as much as the fact that someone in a car could just drive by, fire on them, and continue on his or her way unchecked.

"Not at all," Sprague said. "I like being out in the cold. Keeps the senses alert."

Sydney had meant exposed to sight, not exposed to the weather. She wasn't sure if he was trying to make a joke. Sydney found it hard to believe that he was indifferent to the cold, since he was tightly bundled up in a wool overcoat, a hat, a scarf, and fur-lined gloves. Hardly an inch of his skin was actually *exposed* to the elements. This was going to make her job more difficult.

"Of course, if a tiny bird such as yourself finds it nippy, you can always move a little closer for warmth," he said, holding out an arm.

Sydney ignored the "tiny bird" comment and focused on the flirtation. This would make her ultimate objective easier. She threw in a smile so he would think she was willing to play along. Then she got down to business.

"I hear you have a new shipment of weapons available," Sydney said. "All that you seem to be missing is an interested buyer."

"Oh, I have plenty of interested buyers, Lilia," Sprague said. "But I have yet to find one that interests me."

"I think I can make a very tempting offer," Sydney said. She closed some distance between her and Sprague, as if she had decided to take him up on his offer for warmth. The implication being that she could offer more than money. "But first I'd like to hear about these new Scorpion Pistols."

"You like the name?" Sprague asked. "I came up with it myself. It describes the guns—or the bullets, actually—quite effectively. One sting and your victim is as good as dead."

"Go on," Sydney prodded as she brushed a speck of imaginary dirt off his coat. She allowed her hand to linger on his chest far longer than necessary.

"It fires acid bullets," he explained. "The bullet casing disintegrates on impact, injecting the body with a lethal dose of some rather tenacious flesh-eating acid. Even a minor flesh wound would have devastating results."

"Genius," Sydney said, trying to sound impressed while feeling disgusted. The ways people found to kill each other were truly revolting to her.

"I can't recall the name of the acid," Sprague said with a dismissive wave, "but it doesn't really matter. I shouldn't tell you, anyway. It wouldn't be profitable to give away all my secrets."

"I would love to meet the person who could create such a device," Sydney said, meaning it in so many ways.

"You and half the world market," Sprague said

as he pulled away momentarily. "But that is not part of the deal."

Sydney leaned in close to his ear. "You have yet to hear my offer."

He looked in her eyes for a moment, clearly trying to judge what she had meant by that. Sydney could tell by his expression that he wasn't quite ready to go along with her plan yet. She tried to slide her hand up under his scarf, but he pulled away with a playful smirk.

"Don't you just love the Kindlifresserbrunnen?" Sprague asked, with the heavy word tumbling over his lips. He turned away from Sydney and took several steps toward the fountain. He didn't bother to look back to see if she was following. "Such power in the statue."

Sydney tried not to laugh as she realized what was going on. Maximilian "Maxie" Sprague was trying hard to come off like a B-movie villain. As if it were something to aspire to.

"You like power, don't you?" Sydney asked, deciding to play along so the man could live out his little fantasy.

"I like money," he said. "And the power that it brings."

"Then we should get down to business," Sydney said, pulling him back toward her. "I'm ready to pay double your asking—"

"Phoenix! Get down!" Vaughn's voice yelled in her ear.

Sydney pushed Sprague out of the way and dove for cover behind the fountain. She barely registered the fact that Sprague's guard—now only twenty feet away—had suddenly dropped to the ground. She could tell by the way he had fallen that he wouldn't be getting up anytime soon, if at all.

She looked back to the other guard and saw that he had his gun out and aimed across the street. Looking up, she could see the tip of Vaughn's gun out the window pointed in roughly the same direction. She hadn't heard any shots, but that didn't mean someone wasn't shooting at them.

Sprague's remaining guard suddenly crumpled. Again, she heard nothing, meaning the sniper was using either a tranq gun or a regular pistol with a silencer. Somehow she expected the would-be assassin wasn't into tranquilizers.

Vaughn's gun was also equipped with a silencer, so she wasn't even sure if he had a lock on the sniper and was firing back. She *could* tell

11

that the sniper was now firing at her and Sprague. She felt the sting of concrete and plaster as pieces of the Ogre Fountain came chipping off around her as the bullets struck only a few feet away.

"Stay down!" Sydney said as she grabbed Sprague by the neck. She held him to the ground with her left hand as her right swung up with her gun.

"That grip is a little tight," Sprague moaned from his position face down on the cement. She had her hand wrapped around his neck.

Sydney ignored him. She was too busy trying to do several things at once.

There was a break in the firing. At least, the plaster chips had stopped raining down on them. Sydney leaned low behind the fountain as her eyes scanned across the street. She could see movement behind the trees but couldn't make out the identity of the person. The figure could have been male or female. Tall or short. The one thing she could tell was that the body was moving away.

"I've got nothing," Vaughn said into her ear. "No clear shot on the shooter."

Sydney could understand his problem. From his vantage point he'd only see the tops of the trees. He didn't even have the sound of the gunfire to work from. If the guards hadn't dropped, they wouldn't have even known there was a shooter until it was too late. She couldn't help but wonder why the shooter hadn't just taken Sprague or her out first.

"Cover me," she whispered into her pin.

"What?" Sprague asked with his mouth still pressed to the ground. "What was that?"

Sydney didn't bother to clarify that she wasn't speaking to him. She also didn't wait for Vaughn to warn her against doing what she was about to do. An unexpected opportunity had arisen, and she had to move quickly.

She slipped out from behind the fountain, staying in a crouch with her gun leading the way. For the first time, she was glad that it was a cold winter day, since it kept the innocent tourists indoors. Of course, with fewer people walking, more were on the road taking public transportation. When she saw another trolley coming down the opposite side of the street, she knew she could use it to her advantage.

The small red trolley slowed as Sydney stepped off the curb. Keeping the vehicle in front of her,

Sydney bolted across the street, staying low to the ground. She was torn between relief that the trolley was providing cover and concern that it was dropping off a civilian who didn't know what he or she was getting out in the middle of.

"Anything?" Sydney asked into her comm as she checked the other side of the street through the trolley's windows.

"Nothing," Vaughn replied. "Looks like the shooting has stopped. Sprague's still alive. He keeps popping his head up like a whack-a-mole game."

"Do you see anyone?"

"No. But the tree line is blocking my view."

"I'm going in," Sydney said, and watched as a man exited the trolley and headed south down the street. She was glad to see that he was moving at a brisk pace, taking himself away from the area quickly. Probably wanting to get back indoors.

Sydney waited for the trolley to roll out before walking up to the sidewalk. She performed a quick sweep up and down the street with her eyes and her gun, but saw no one. Based on how the plaster and concrete had fallen, she assumed that the shooter had been on the north end of the street.

Moving slowly, she now walked along the row of trees searching for any sign of life. She walked farther than she knew the shooter could have been positioned, but found nothing but more empty streets leading off in different directions. The shooter could be anywhere—in any of the buildings or even zipping away in a car. She had lost him.

As she slowly turned back in the direction from which she had come, Sydney noticed something pinned to the tree beside her. It was the size of a credit card and black except for a white spot in the center.

"Looks like someone left us a message," she said to Vaughn over the comm.

Sydney stepped over to the card and pulled it from the tree. It was card-stock paper, like a business card. The white spot in the center was actually a star with the number thirteen written in the middle in black. It was definitely a message, but Sydney didn't know what it meant.

She pocketed the card for further examination later and filled Vaughn in on the find. After one last sweep of the area, she hurried back across the street. Sprague was waiting for her, standing, by the fountain. He had obviously grown bored of hiding on the ground. Sydney was almost upset to think that she had probably scared off the shooter before he could finish the job.

"Maybe you should start doing business indoors," Sydney said as she returned to the task at hand. Her mission was largely accomplished, but she had to complete the deal to get out of there without raising suspicion. "A nice quiet coffee-house, perhaps?"

"Then they'd just poison my drink," Sprague said, without bothering to ask about the shooter. He seemed bored by the turn of events, but Sydney could tell it was an act. She suspected *his* shivering wasn't just due to the cold. But a true B-movie villain would never let anyone get to him. "It's the price of business in my line of work."

Sydney could see that Vaughn was still keeping watch from the third-story window, for whatever good it was doing. Whoever had been there was gone. The message had been delivered, though she wasn't sure if it was meant for her or for Sprague. She wasn't about to tip her hand by asking him about it.

"Speaking of business," Sydney said, looking back at the dead guards. She seemed to be the only one concerned about them.

"Double my asking price, I believe is what you said, Lilia?" Sprague continued the conversation as if they had only been interrupted by someone asking for directions.

"Yes," she confirmed.

"Sounds fair," he said, considering the offer. "But why don't we knock five percent off that? For saving my life."

He held out his gloved hand and Sydney took it. "I think we have a deal," she said, ignoring the fact that he was squeezing a little too tightly. Sydney gave him one last smile.

"It has been a true pleasure doing business with you," he said. "Perhaps we can meet again sometime?"

"Perhaps," Sydney said, knowing she didn't sound as eager as she was supposed to be acting. She could only carry this alias so far.

"I mean, for business, of course," he said. "I have something in development that you might find of interest."

"Do tell," Sydney prodded. She had assumed the meet was over, but he didn't seem to want her to leave. She wasn't sure if the interest was personal or professional, but she figured it would be best to hear him out. It never hurt to know when additional weaponry would be in play.

"I'm afraid I can't offer more than a tease," he said, obviously enjoying the game. "But you should know that I don't go around mentioning it to all of my clients. Just the ones who save my life."

"I'm honored." Sydney played along. "But can you tell me *anything* about it?"

"Well," he said, obviously savoring the moment, "I will say that it is a weapon the likes of which could change the face of the world, as they say."

Sydney tried to pull some more information from Sprague, but he had played his game and said all he intended to say. He wanted to meet her again and was dangling his new toy in front of her as a temptation. Once it was clear she wasn't going to learn anything more, they finalized the arrangements for the shipment of Scorpion Pistols, flirted a little more, and finally parted ways. Sprague didn't even bother to check on the dead guards he left behind.

Sydney hurried into the building as soon as he turned the corner. A police car was coming down the street, and she didn't want to be around when they noticed the bodies lying out on the sidewalk.

VIGILANCE

The meet hadn't gone as planned, but she'd still managed to accomplish both of her goals. Conveniently, the shooter had unknowingly helped her with the more important of the objectives.

CHAPTER 2

LOS ANGELES

"Phase one was a success," Arvin Sloane said as he addressed the team in the glass- and white-walled conference room of the underground headquarters of APO. The black ops CIA unit formally known as Authorized Personnel Only had been in existence for just a short time but had already proven successful on a variety of top secret projects. It wasn't a surprise, considering the caliber of the individuals in the unit, but taking into account the unique work environment, Sydney was amazed that they were managing as well as they were so early in the game.

She still felt odd in the sparsely designed room. It was like working in a fish bowl. On one hand it was unnerving to be in such an open workplace. On the other, it was comforting to know that it would be difficult for anyone involved in clandestine activities to go unnoticed. And considering certain people in the room, there were many opportunities for clandestine activities in the workplace.

"Within the week the U.S. government will be in control of a considerable stock of Scorpion Pistols," Sloane continued, throwing an unnerving smile in Sydney's direction. She had done her job. She didn't need him to point it out for everyone.

It *was* her job, she kept reminding herself. She was supposed to have let Sprague go even though his weapons sales had been responsible for countless deaths across the globe. Even though she knew he was already making more deals that would lead to future deaths.

Sprague's hand was clearly seen in the escalation of certain international conflicts that could easily have been handled through peaceful negotiations. Sydney wasn't naïve enough to think that all conflict could be ended by simple discussion, but she wished smaller governments would give that avenue more of a chance.

Once Sprague's weaponry reached one side of a conflict, the opposing government was sure to put in a matching order, plus ten percent. Keeping up with the Joneses took on a whole new meaning in the global arms race. And not since Ineni Hassan had Sydney met anyone who was so good at turning a profit from it.

"What will be done with the guns?" Nadia Santos asked. She was still asking the questions that Sydney had long since given up on.

"Naturally, they will be destroyed," Sloane replied. "They are . . . unnecessarily vicious weaponry."

Of course, Sloane would know a thing or two about being unnecessarily vicious, considering his personal history. Sydney wished that she could believe him about the guns being destroyed, but something about his voice rang false. Then again, most of what he said sounded like lies to Sydney. She was still coming to terms with working for a man she didn't trust in the least.

"That just leaves a dozen warehouses around the world full of other similarly deadly devices," Vaughn added. "Not to mention this supersecret weapon Sprague mentioned. We should definitely look into that."

"All in due time," Sloane replied. "That is not the goal for today."

Sydney looked about the room, going down the roll call in her mind: Vaughn, Dixon, Marshall, Weiss, Nadia, and Sydney's own father, Jack. She had become close friends with each of them over the years, through a series of unexpected working relationships. None of them had any reason to trust Arvin Sloane. In fact, they all had every reason in the world *not* to trust him. And yet here they were working under him.

Sydney pushed that thought out of her mind. She had already spent numerous sleepless nights thinking about the decision that had teamed her with her sworn enemy. She had made her decision, and dwelling on it wasn't going to change anything. At least she wasn't alone. At one time or another Sloane had betrayed just about every member of the team, to varying degrees of horror.

It seemed like a joke that anyone—let alone the U.S. government—would authorize Arvin Sloane to have control over a lemonade stand, much less a highly secret organization working against the same forms of global terrorism he had once overseen as the head of SD-6. But, again, that bed had been made, and Sydney was already lying between the sheets.

At least now Sydney was on the side of the government. Even though she had intended to resign from the CIA several times, Sydney couldn't help but feel that continuing with intelligence work was at least some penance for her past actions. Sure, she hadn't been aware of her involvement in illegal activities when she was at SD-6, but she still felt like she hadn't really made up for the things she had unknowingly done back then.

Today, at least, she *believed* she was on the right side. She wasn't entirely sure of that when she had to let someone like Maximilian Sprague go on his merry way. She kept reminding herself that her actions served the greater good. Even when it didn't seem that way.

"What about Martine?" Sydney asked, trying to focus on the point of the mission. She had let Sprague walk away for a reason, after all. She was ready for phase two to begin. "Sprague shut me down when I tried to ask about his weapons designer. When will we know more about her?"

"Hopefully soon," Jack Bristow said. The look on her father's face signaled that she needed to calm down. Apparently, she hadn't managed to keep the impatience out of her voice when she had asked the question. She honestly didn't mind if anyone had taken notice.

"Yes," Sloane added. "I suspect we should be determining her location shortly, thanks to you, Sydney."

He's up to something, Sydney thought.

Sloane had been heaping exaggerated praise on her for weeks in a rather transparent attempt to win her over since she'd joined APO. Today he was really turning it on. She remained stone-faced to silently let him know that it wasn't working.

Sloane held her glare for a moment before moving on. "Marshall."

"Um . . . yes, hi," Marshall said with a wave as he stood. He often came across like the kid in class who was surprised the teacher had called on him even though he knew every answer. The technological genius was a bundle of energy who could drive many people insane with his rambling. Sydney couldn't help but love him as a dear friend despite—and because of—his quirks.

"The Second-Skin Tracker that Sydney impressively managed to slip onto the back of Sprague's neck—and I don't think I've mentioned how cool it was that you could slip it onto him, under his scarf, without him noticing, while you were being shot at—is working perfectly."

Sydney tried to wrap her mind around that sentence, but gave up halfway through.

"Second Skin?" Nadia asked. She had missed the earlier brief because of some paperwork she needed to complete for Langley. There seemed to be no end to the red tape involved in her transfer from Argentinean Intelligence to the APO team. Sydney couldn't help but worry that reams of paperwork were counterproductive for members of a black ops team. But that was government work in a nutshell.

Marshall's eyes immediately lit up when he realized that not only Nadia but Weiss and Dixon had missed the earlier brief. The only thing that excited Marshall more than talking about new technology was talking about his son, Mitchell. And if he could manage to fit both into the same conversation, he was overjoyed.

"Just one of my latest brilliant inventions,"

Marshall said with forced immodesty. He pulled what looked like a small piece of flesh out of his jacket pocket. "Oh, look, I just happen to have an early prototype with me in case someone asked."

Sydney tried not to look at Vaughn. She knew if their eyes met they would both start laughing. Marshall's act was always something to be appreciated and enjoyed. Unless you were her father or Sloane, that is. They were often the first to cut him off as his discussion veered to some oddly humorous place. But even they indulged Marshall on occasion.

"This tiny little strip of synthetic human skin is actually a tracking device," Marshall explained. "The one placed on Sprague has been sending his location to a satellite since the moment Syd placed it on him. We can track him through our GPS system. And the best thing is, once this little guy is attached to the skin, it is virtually undetectable."

"Wait a minute," Weiss said. "He's not going to notice he has a Band-Aid stuck on his neck?"

Marshall looked offended, but Sydney knew Weiss was just baiting the technician to brag a bit more. "This is a state-of-the-art combination of latex, microtechnology, and animal flesh," he said.

"Not some mass-produced cloth bandage. Here, give me your hand."

Marshall didn't wait for Weiss. Instead he grabbed the agent's hand and held it out, palm down.

"Careful," Weiss said with a mock flirtatious tone. "You're a married man."

Marshall ignored the comment and slipped the Second Skin onto the back of Weiss's right hand. "Now you tell me Johnson & Johnson can come up with anything like that."

"Wow, I can't feel it at all," Weiss said as he rubbed his left hand over the patch, then held it out to look at. "I can't see it either."

"Naturally," Marshall said as he removed the prototype. "I designed it to mimic the exact shade of the subject's flesh. The Second Skin will eventually wash off Sprague's neck, in about three days. So long as the he bathes regularly, which I assume he does. I mean, I don't sit around wondering about his personal grooming habits. . . . I'm still working on a stronger adhesive. I figure one of these may come in handy by the time Mitchell starts driving."

Marshall paused. Sydney knew he was waiting for the right question to further explain his genius. She figured that she would provide it if no one else did.

"But how will that get us to Martine?" Dixon asked. "What if they don't meet in person in the next three days? Where are we tracking him to?"

"I'm glad you asked," Marshall said, holding the tiny piece of latex and animal flesh to the light.

"You're probably thinking, 'Marshall has designed much smaller tracking devices, so what's so special about this one?' Right?" Marshall looked around the room like a magician making sure the audience was paying attention to his trick. Except, in this case, he *was* going to explain the secrets of his magic.

"This tiny technology," he continued, "also contains a device that will record every conversation Maximilian Sprague has over the next three days. Those conversations will be compressed into a data stream and eventually sent via burst transmissions to a satellite at prescribed intervals throughout each day. The satellite will bounce the compressed conversations here, where we will decompress the recording and listen in on everything he said. It's not live, but it's not quite Memorex, either."

Marshall looked quite satisfied with himself.

"But why send burst transmissions?" Weiss asked. "Could we just put a bug on him that was set to continuous transmission?"

Marshall deflated a bit. "Oh, sure, if you wanted to get caught," he said. "For someone so laid back, Sprague has surprisingly tight security protocols. I think it has something to do with Stefani Martine. Rumor has it she's a freak when it comes to security. Anyway, a continuous transmission could easily be traced. It was hard enough to develop a tracking signal that could be hidden. You want me to do that with an actual voice recording, it's gonna cost you." He looked at Sloane. "Not that I'm complaining about my current rate of pay. It's just . . . well . . . with a young child at home and Carrie talking about maybe wanting another . . . I don't want to imply that when I joined—"

"Marshall," Sloane said.

Marshall turned back to Weiss. "Besides, how much battery life do you think I can fit into this thing?" he asked. "I'm good, but I'm not that good. The burst transmission takes up less power." Then he mumbled under his breath. "I mean, I'm not perfect, you know. I'm only human. Sure, when I give you exactly what you need you're all, 'Marshall you're amazing,' but today—"

"Stefani Martine," Sloane announced, putting an end to Marshall's rambling. Sloane hit a button on the keypad in front of him and the image of a dark-haired woman in her midforties came up on the computer screens that lined the wall of the conference room.

"Yowza," Marshall said under his breath. He'd reacted the same way the first time her image had appeared on the screen at the prior briefing two days earlier. Even Sydney had to admit that Martine's sharp, angular features only added to the woman's beauty.

"We expect Sprague to make contact with Martine to discuss Sydney's order of Scorpion Pistols. And possibly this new device he mentioned. Be ready to move when we get confirmation of her location. There's a safe house waiting once we get her in the States."

"I'd like to go on record that I have issues with this plan," Sydney said.

"Yes, Sydney," Sloane replied with a note of exasperation in his voice. "You made your objections perfectly clear during the initial brief. This is the plan Langley approved."

"Because you pushed for it," Sydney reminded him. "Stefani Martine belongs in prison."

"That would do no one any good," Sloane said.

"She has been responsible for countless deaths," Sydney said. There wasn't any chance she was going to convince Sloane to change the plan, but it didn't mean she couldn't make her opinion known. "Her weapons have been used in everything from assassinations to full-scale wars. And she keeps coming up with new ways to kill people. She has to be stopped."

"But why stop her when we can have her on our side?" Sloane reasoned.

It's that kind of logic that keeps the world a breath away from war every day, Sydney thought.

"A person like that can't be trusted," Sydney insisted, not caring to hide the fact that she wasn't just referring to Stefani Martine.

"Of course she can," Sloane said. "We just have to make the right offer. I think a lifetime of . . . well . . . *life* as opposed to the death penalty is a good starting point."

"And if she doesn't take the deal?" Vaughn asked, obviously trying, in his own way, to support Sydney while moving the conversation forward.

"She'll take the deal," Jack said, obviously siding with Sloane. Sydney tried not to take it personally. Her father often had an easier time dealing with the shadier side of their business.

"How do you know that?" Nadia asked.

"Marshall?" Jack looked to the technician.

"Yeah—um—yes?"

"What's the one punishment worse than the death penalty for you?" Jack asked.

"Taking my wife and son," Marshall said without hesitation.

Sydney noticed that her father looked as if he hadn't expected that answer. It was only a brief shift in his facial features. Most people wouldn't have noticed the hesitation, but it wasn't lost on her.

"And after that?" Jack pressed on. "What would be the worst thing anyone could do to you?"

Marshall looked confused, like he was worried about getting the answer wrong. "Well, I didn't like it that time I was tortured," Marshall said with a shiver. "But the absolute worst thing I can imagine is someone telling me I couldn't do my work anymore. I mean, I'd, like, explode if I couldn't build all this—"

"Exactly," Sloane jumped in. "Stefani Martine has more than enough money to live several lives of leisure. She only continues to work because she loves what she does."

Sydney managed to suppress a snort of disgust as Sloane continued.

"Martine will only be allowed to continue her weapons development if she agrees to do it for us."

"Don't you mean 'for the U.S. government'?" Sydney asked.

Sloane's face fell into that smug, self-satisfied look that Sydney had long since learned to hate. "That is what I said."

"So now we just sit around and wait?" Dixon asked.

"What about that card Sydney found?" Vaughn asked. "With the star and the number thirteen?"

"Yes. The mysterious card," Jack said as he punched a button on his remote control and an image of the business card appeared on the screen. "We believe it is the symbol for a group known as the Thirteen Stars."

"Thirteen Stars?" Sydney repeated. Her mind immediately went to the original colonies and Betsy Ross's flag. "Does that mean they're based here? In America?"

"So far as we can tell," Jack said. "According to the CIA files we accessed, they have received very little information on the organization from the

FBI. Of course, the FBI says they have turned over all their records in the new spirit of cooperation between agencies."

"Then what is Thirteen Stars doing attacking an Austrian man in Switzerland?" Vaughn wondered aloud.

"We're not sure," Jack said. "Thirteen Stars is rumored to have been behind several assassination attempts on foreign dignitaries while on U.S. soil."

"It should be mentioned," Sloane added, "that these so-called 'dignitaries' tended to be those with, shall we say . . . *strained* relationships with the U.S."

"Of course none of these assassination attempts have been successful," Jack said. "But they have managed to stir up trouble, bringing some of the government's shadier dealings to light. I should mention that nothing has been found to link the organization to the attempts. It's all speculation at this point."

"What about the calling card?" Sydney asked.

"This is the first time one has been found," Jack said. "We're not even sure that it refers to this Thirteen Stars organization. It just seems likely from a statistical standpoint."

"They don't seem like much of a concern," Weiss

said. "I mean, they keep missing their targets."

"Do they?" Sloane wondered aloud. "Just because the intended target is still alive doesn't mean that a message hasn't been sent."

"Why do we think they went after Sprague?" Dixon asked.

"It's likely they were unhappy with a deal that went sour," Sloane said. "Sprague told Sydney that he had many buyers interested in the Scorpion Pistols. And Sprague has been known to change his mind in the middle of negotiations. He's made more than a few enemies that way."

"The larger concern is the business card," Jack said. "After a few years of almost obsessively clandestine activities, it seems like Thirteen Stars wants to go public. We're not sure exactly what that means at this point. We assume they have something big planned. It's possible Sprague fits into that plan."

Sydney considered the ramifications of what Jack was saying. If it was a terrorist organization working inside U.S. borders, it technically fell under the purview of the FBI and the Department of Homeland Security. Even the attempt on Sprague could be handled by the traditional CIA offices. Certainly Thirteen Stars had done nothing so far that warranted the interest of the black ops team. Somehow, Sydney didn't think they had seen the last of the organization, though.

The meeting broke up on Jack's unsettling comment. There was plenty of work to do while they waited to find the location of Stefani Martine. Marshall said that the burst transmission should come in shortly, so everyone needed to be on alert until then.

Sydney left the conference room, hoping to bury her head in some work for a while. As she left, she noticed that Sloane had asked Nadia to stay behind for a moment. Sydney did not think it was work related. She and her newly found sister had grown closer in the short time they had lived together, but there was still some distance between them, particularly in areas related to Sloane. Even with those differences, Sydney expected that whatever Sloane was discussing with his daughter, Sydney would find out soon enough.

CHAPTER 3

After determining that the shooter had
left the area, I returned to Sprague,
that cocky little

Delete. Delete. Delete.

. . . I returned to find Sprague.
The low-life scum didn't even care
that his two guards

Delete. Delete. Delete.

Sydney sat at her desk, staring at the computer screen. She wanted to throw something, but the open design of the APO offices kept her from lashing out. It wasn't like she could shut her door and lock out the world, as much as she wanted to at the moment.

Her mission report was taking longer to write than usual. She was having an especially difficult time keeping emotion out of the report and simply sticking to the facts. This wasn't the first time this had happened to her over the years. She knew it wouldn't be the last.

"Let me guess," Vaughn said as he came over and leaned on the edge of her desk. "Second thoughts about teaming with Sloane."

"Actually, I think I'm up to the millionth thoughts," Sydney replied, taking a break from her work. "But that's not today's issue."

"I'll bite," Vaughn said. "What part of our crazy lives is getting you down?"

Sydney checked the open area to make sure no one was listening. She could only assume their boss didn't have the entire place bugged. "I've spent so much time agonizing over my decision to work with Sloane that I've lost track of the smaller picture."

"Smaller picture?" Vaughn asked.

"The everyday evil we work with," Sydney said. "Letting Sprague go. Trying to make a deal with Martine. It's like we're not in the business to stop the bad guys. We want to get in bed with them."

"I assume this would be a bad place to make a joke about getting into bed?" Vaughn asked, obviously trying to lighten the dark subject.

Sydney gave him a tired look. "Why couldn't we take Sprague in and force him to tell us Martine's location?"

"Just beat it out of him?" Vaughn said lightly.

"That's one option," Sydney said. She immediately wondered when she had started playfully joking about torture. Normal people didn't do that kind of thing. Or, if they did, they weren't involved in a world where torturing people was a reality. "He's a greedy businessman. There are any number of ways to get the information out of him."

"Stefani Martine *is* his business," Vaughn reminded her. "Without Martine he's simply moving existing shipments. There's no real money in that. Sprague wouldn't give up his main source of income that easily. We'll get him soon enough."

"Will we?" Sydney wondered aloud. "And how

many deals will he make before we *do* get him? How many people will die?"

"We'll make a huge dent in his business when we convince Martine to work for us," Vaughn said. "Sometimes we have to focus on the minor victories."

"I don't know about you," Sydney said, "but I got into this to put an end to evil, not put a 'dent' in it."

And how's that going so far? she silently asked herself.

"Hey, I'm on your side, remember," Vaughn said. He threw up his hands in a mock defensive gesture.

"Sorry," Sydney said. She really did feel bad about attacking him. It wasn't his fault she had decided to get deeper into black ops. She hadn't even consulted him before she joined APO. Not that they were on the closest terms at the time. They had both gone through some insanity just before they had made their decisions to sign up. Even though she hadn't known Sloane was part of the equation when she agreed to come in, Sydney had been aware that the team would be working outside of the law from time to time. But knowing and actually doing were two entirely different things.

"You can't let it get to you," Vaughn said. "Sometimes it's necessary to bend the rules."

"Says the former Boy Scout," Sydney said, recalling his previous CIA handle.

"I am never going to live that down," Vaughn said, shaking his head. "But you know what I mean. If there's something we've both learned over the years, it's that sometimes we do have to focus on the greater good."

"True," Sydney relented. "But at what cost?"

Vaughn didn't have an answer for her, but Sydney hadn't really been expecting one. They sat together in silence for a moment, simply being there emotionally for each other. Unfortunately, the moment was all too public, and all too brief.

"Am I interrupting?" Nadia asked as she stepped up to Sydney's desk.

Nadia was still getting comfortable working in the APO offices. Even though everyone else on the team had been on alternate sides over the years, they had a shared history. Sydney and Dixon were old partners. She and her father had teamed with Vaughn and Weiss several years back. The rest of

them had been working together to some degree
since the fall of SD-6. Nadia was the unknown element and still occasionally entered conversations
with apologies.

"No. What is it?" Sydney asked. There was a
clear look of discomfort on Nadia's face. Considering
the complex web of personal and professional issues
they dealt with in the workplace, Sydney braced herself for anything.

"I don't know, really," Nadia said, obviously
searching for the right words.

"I'll let you two talk," Vaughn said, sensing the
tense mood.

"Oh, no, it's—," Nadia started to say, but
stopped herself. It was clear that she wanted a
moment alone with her sister.

"Weiss may need help researching Stefani
Martine," Vaughn said, and quickly moved away.

Sydney looked at Nadia, waiting for her to
speak. Sydney had just recently stopped referring
to Nadia as her "half sister" and embraced her
fully as a sister. Sure there were still secrets
between the two of them, including one rather
large one at the moment regarding the death of
their mother. They were still learning to live with

each other, but it was getting easier with every passing day. Then there came times like these when Sydney suspected that Nadia needed a sister more than anything else. And she was glad to be there to fill the need.

"Let's go get some coffee," Sydney said as she grabbed her purse and her pager and took her sister by the arm.

"What about Martine?" Nadia asked. "Marshall said the first transmission from Sprague was coming in."

"They'll page us," Sydney said. Suddenly she really needed to get out of the office and get some fresh air. "We won't be far."

The two women slipped out of APO unnoticed. It wasn't like they were trapped inside the office once they entered, but Sydney didn't want Sloane to see them sneaking out. She preferred to keep her relationship with Nadia separate from her relationship with Sloane. It wouldn't help if he knew that Nadia was coming to her after Nadia's private conversation with him. Sydney assumed that's what this was about.

They could have stayed in the office and sat in the break room. The coffee there was perfectly fine for a workplace beverage. But being in L.A., there was a coffeehouse on every corner, and Sydney found personal conversations were so much easier when she wasn't within the bright white walls of APO, wondering who could be listening.

Conveniently, the small mom-and-pop coffee-house wasn't overly busy. It was crowded but not with the huge L.A. coffee masses that the chain shops usually attracted. Once they put in their order, Nadia searched for a table while Sydney waited for the drinks. Sydney had ordered a frozen-caramel-and-chocolate concoction and didn't hesi-tate when offered a whipped cream topping. She figured she'd probably have the chance to work off the calories soon enough.

Nadia's order was less interesting. A simple Café Americano, which was light on the extras and subsequently only a couple dollars, as opposed to Sydney's four-dollar creation.

With drinks in hand Sydney realized Nadia must have found seats outside. All of the interior tables were taken. Each table hosted a lone person—most of them male—with a laptop. So many of the city's aspiring writers spent their days in coffeehouses downing their lattes while creating their magnum opuses. Sydney imagined that the drug-inspired writers of the sixties probably got a kick out of today's writers, who sought inspiration from the mind-altering effects of caffeine.

Sydney pushed through the glass door into the sunny L.A. morning. The city was experiencing one of its many midwinter warm spells, so different from Switzerland's current cold snap. It was the kind of weather that had allowed her to host a barbecue on the patio for her New Year's Eve party. It was the reason why, no matter where in the world she traveled, she always came home to L.A.

"So, what's wrong?" Sydney asked as she slid into the waiting empty chair and handed Nadia her Café Americano.

"It's nothing, really," Nadia said as she removed the plastic lid to let the drink cool. "Nothing. It's just . . . Mr. Sloane . . . Arvin . . . my father . . ."

Sydney remembered all too well a time when she didn't know what to call her own father. After years of estrangement they had finally fallen into a comfortable relationship. Sure, there were still times when the pressures of their lives interfered. They had just come out of another time of stress in the relationship. But at the end of the day Sydney knew that he loved her unconditionally.

But Sydney had known her father her entire life. More to the point, Jack Bristow had known that he had a daughter since she was born. For Sloane this was a fairly recent development. For Nadia, even more recent. As if the simple act of a reunion didn't have enough emotional land mines, the reality of this particular situation would have been almost too much to bear.

Nadia had trailed off on the conversation. It was clear she was trying to figure out the best way to say whatever was on her mind. Sydney knew that she didn't make it easy for Nadia to talk about Sloane. It wasn't like Sydney was intentionally trying to hurt her sister. She just had trouble discussing that particular subject.

Sydney took a sip of her frozen drink to give her sister some time to collect her thoughts. After a minute of silence she decided to help the conversation along.

"Hey, whatever it is," Sydney said, "I promise not to fly off the handle. Well, not too much."

Nadia smiled and pressed on. "Apparently, at the start of every year Omnifam gives a big presentation to all its employees and the media. The presentation reviews Omnifam's humanitarian efforts of the previous year and outlines the plan for the next year."

"I think I can see where this is going," Sydney said, trying for levity but not quite making it.

"Even though he stepped down as the day-to-day head of Omnifam," Nadia continued, "my father has been invited to be the keynote speaker at the event. They're going to host it in Los Angeles, but it will be broadcast to the 'global Omnifam family,' according to him. It's supposed to be some big multimedia event with speakers and video. There's even talk that U2 may perform."

Nadia paused, leaving Sydney to fill in the blanks. Even though she'd had a year to get used to it, Sydney was still amazed by Sloane's ability to reinvent himself for the public.

"And he wants you there as part of *his* family?" Sydney asked. She knew that Nadia wanted to take things slowly with getting to know her father, but Sydney wasn't surprised that Sloane was ignoring his daughter's wishes.

"It's not like he wants to parade me onstage and make some announcement," Nadia said. "He just wants me to attend. He promised that he wouldn't introduce me to anyone as his daughter. He'd just call me a business associate."

Even when he's trying to do something right, it comes out so wrong, Sydney thought, but chose not to say anything. She couldn't remain totally silent, however. "I don't mean to be harsh," Sydney said, "but you know why he's doing this, right?"

"So that I see him trying to make up for his past," Nadia replied. "I know you don't think he's changed."

"I don't," Sydney gently agreed. As far as she was concerned, this was just another chapter in the Arvin Sloane Book of Redemption. "But I'm not going to stop you from trying to connect with him. You're being careful."

"I am," Nadia said.

"But . . ."

"It's going to be kind of overwhelming," Nadia said. "A hall full of people who see my father as a purely virtuous benefactor. Carried live to the 'global Omnifam family.' None of whom know anything about his sordid past."

"You want someone there to help provide balance?" Sydney surmised.

"To keep me from getting too wrapped up in it,"

Nadia confirmed. "You don't need to really do anything. Just be there for me. Someone who won't be fawning all over him like he's the second coming."

Sydney was used to playing devil's advocate when it came to the idea of a reformed Sloane, but it was still odd to be asked to formally step into that position. She could understand why Nadia needed the perspective. This presentation combined with his recent acceptance of a humanitarian award from the UN showed that he was intent on continuing to rehabilitate his reputation. It made sense that Nadia wanted to keep things in perspective. Sydney just didn't know whether she would be able to sit through the event without being totally sickened.

"It's an early morning thing because of the time difference with Omnifam headquarters," Nadia said. "So we could go for breakfast afterward. My treat."

Sydney knew that she should say yes. Nadia wasn't really asking for much, when it came down to it. It wasn't as if Sydney didn't have to listen to Sloane on a daily basis, anyway. But there was something about taking part in Sloane's act that bothered Sydney. It was just one more part of her that would be giving in. One more step into the dark side, as it were.

"He put me on the guest list as me plus one," Nadia said. "I figure he thought it would be easier on me if I brought someone along."

Before Sydney could answer, both of their cell phones started vibrating. Both of the screens bore the same coded text message. APO had found Martine.

Sydney and Nadia left the coffeehouse without finishing their conversation. Sydney knew that she just had to give a simple yes or no, but for some reason she couldn't bring herself to say either. At least they could table the conversation until after the mission. It wasn't as though they could do anything about it until they got back from wherever in the world they were about to be sent.

CHAPTER 4

Sydney and Nadia were the last to enter the APO conference room. Sydney couldn't help but notice Sloane's curious glance her way. Instead of returning the look, she focused her attention on the seat she was about to take. It was bad enough Sloane knew that Nadia had come to her, presumably to ask Sydney to join in at the event he was hosting. She didn't need to give him any indication that she still wasn't sure if she was going to go.

The short walk back from the coffeehouse had been a little uncomfortable, as it had been clear by that point that Sydney was stalling. She still hadn't managed to give Nadia an answer. On the bright side, the page had come at a good time. Sydney could only imagine trying to stall while they were sitting at their table finishing their coffees. At least now she had work to keep her from coming up with an answer.

"We got information off the Second Skin?" Sydney asked once she sat.

"Of course," Marshall said. "It worked perfectly. . . . Well, maybe not *entirely* perfectly. We managed to record Sprague's conversation with Stefani Martine. The transmission came as scheduled. But the tracking device went dead shortly after the transmission ended. It was supposed to last for two more transmissions. I think it may have overloaded. I mean, all that technology in an itty-bitty piece of fleshlike substance." He held up the prototype again. "Even I can't—"

"And the recording led to Martine?" Dixon gently guided the conversation back on course.

"Yes," Marshall said as he accessed the recording through the conference room computers. "But they also talk about something else that may be of interest. Listen and learn."

After a brief moment of dead air, the recording kicked in.

"My dear Martine, I have missed you so." Sprague's voice came through the conference-room speakers. Sydney was slightly unnerved by the now familiar voice. The transmission was so clear that it was almost as if he were in the room. And he was still playing up the B-movie bad-guy image he was working so hard to cultivate.

"Bonjour, Maxie," a woman's slightly muffled voice replied. Sydney was seriously impressed that they picked up the other end of the phone conversation as well. She knew that Sprague was left-handed, so there was a good chance he held his phone to his left ear. When she'd placed the Second Skin on him, Marshall had suggested that she place it as close to his ear as possible, in the hope they could pick up any phone calls. Still, Sydney hadn't expected to be able to record Martine's voice so clearly.

"I hope you are enjoying the sun and the sea," Sprague replied. "Although I'd like to think you're working more than living it up."

"And who ever said there isn't time to do both?" Martine replied, using a forced jovial tone.

Even through the phone and over the recording, Sydney could hear that Martine had a slight edge to her voice as she spoke to Sprague. It was nice to know that she wasn't the only one annoyed by his manner.

"Yes," Sprague replied. "And speaking of which, it looks like we have a buyer for the Scorpions. A perfectly lovely woman with a beauty that is only rivaled by her bank account."

Sydney nearly laughed at the odd compliment. She could see that Vaughn and Weiss were also stifling their giggles. Her father look unmoved as usual.

"Well, make sure to wire me my cut," Martine said abruptly, as if she wanted to end the call. "If that's all—"

"Actually, no!" Sprague said quickly so he wouldn't be cut off. "I was wondering how you are coming on that . . . special project." Sydney swore she could almost see Sprague checking to make sure no one was listening before he said "special project."

"Swimmingly," Martine replied.

Sydney assumed that this was the weapon he had teased her with in Bern. She figured this was the real reason for his call. From the brief conversation Sydney had heard so far, Martine didn't seem all that interested in the day-to-day business Sprague conducted. She came across as more of a send-me-the-money-and-leave-me-alone kind of person. It was clear Sprague was using the sale as a pretense to initiate a conversation about this weapon.

"I know many buyers who would be very interested if I could start leaking word on the development," Sprague said. "*Very* interested."

"It's a bit premature," Martine said. "Maybe next week."

"But you said that last week," Sprague replied, sounding less congenial than Sydney had ever heard in her limited dealings with the man. "I'm beginning to wonder if maybe you've completed the device and are working a separate deal on your own."

"And where would I find a buyer out here?" Martine laughed. Sydney could tell the laugh was added just to upset Sprague.

"I think I'd like to see just how far you've gotten on the final component," Sprague said.

"But we don't dock for three days," Martine replied.

"Well, then, maybe I'll just come out to see you," Sprague said. "I've been feeling in need of a vacation recently."

There was a short pause. "I'm looking forward to it," Martine replied. "Now I must get back to work."

"Lovely speaking with you," Sprague said.

"And you as well, Maxie," Martine replied, not sounding like she meant it in the least. Maybe it would be easier to convince her to work for the government than Sydney had thought. Part of her still hoped that Martine would refuse so they could lock her away for good, though.

Marshall stopped the recording. "We also heard Sprague doing some other business, which we're looking into—planning to 'compensate' the families of his dead bodyguards, and spending an evening with a female companion. I gotta tell you, those are always so uncomfortable to overhear. Even worse when there's video, too. I mean, talk about personal business."

"They won't dock for three days?" Dixon asked, bringing the conversation back on track. "Does Martine own a yacht?"

"You caught that too?" Marshall asked. "No yacht that we could find. However, from that salient little detail we were able to tap into some 'not so public' records and trace Stefani Martine here." He pushed a button on the computer screen in front of him. The image of a huge ocean liner popped up on the wall of video screens.

"That's some boat," Weiss said.

"Technically, it's a ship," Marshall said. "You know, a boat would be like that little clown fish in *Finding Nemo*. You know, the cute little white and orange guy. Mitchell just loves that movie. He can watch it over and over and over—"

"I was kidding, Marshall," Weiss said. "I know the difference."

"The *Triton*," Sloane interrupted, returning to the subject. "A residential liner."

"Residential?" Vaughn asked.

"One of only two in existence," Sloane said. He punched a button on his handheld remote, and various images of the *Triton*'s apartment-style staterooms filled the screens. "A floating tax shelter registered in the Bahamas but traveling the world."

"Wait a minute," Sydney interrupted. "A weapons designer who routinely works with nitro and C-4 and any number of other combustible materials has a *floating* lab?"

This seemed crazier to Sydney than the Ogre Fountain tourist attraction.

"We think she has properties all over the world," Weiss said. Sydney knew that while she had been in Switzerland, he had been reading up on Martine and compiling useable information. "Labs. Warehouses. We think she even has an office in the Pacific Design Center a few miles from here. She probably does all the actual construction and testing of the bombs, guns, and other goodies in her land-based operations and just uses her lab for designing. Maybe preliminary construction. Certainly nothing with high explosives. Martine is obsessive about safety . . . and security."

"But she can only get to her labs when the ship docks?" Sydney asked. "Then how is Sprague going to get to her?"

Sloane hit another button on the remote that showed the top deck of the ship. "The *Triton* has a functioning helipad. Considering the cost of the residential properties, the cruise company makes sure that their clientele can have access to the ship wherever it is in the world."

"The *Triton*'s residents range from the world's wealthiest and most respected heads of business to some of the more nefarious underworld figures," Jack said.

"Or, in some cases, both," Marshall added. "With the wealthy it's so hard to tell these days."

Not just with the wealthy, Sydney thought.

"The ship is currently located off the coast of Peru," Jack continued, "and traveling through the South Pacific. We know that Sprague is flying into Lima and then taking a helicopter out to meet Martine. We don't know if he plans to take her off the ship when he leaves or if he really is just stopping by, as he says."

"Which means we must intercept Martine before Sprague can fly from Switzerland to Peru," Sloane said. "We must make contact and convince her that we can offer a more secure position with the U.S. government than she has in Sprague's organization."

"Or she spends the rest of her life in jail," Sydney added.

"We feel that she would prefer the alternative," Sloane replied. "However, we need a contingency to make sure she doesn't hold too much bargaining power. Therefore, while we make contact with our offer, Marshall will secure her computer so we can procure the information on her current designs."

"Including this special project Sprague keeps talking about," Nadia added.

"We hope so," Vaughn added. "Like Weiss said, Martine is obsessive about security. We've gone through some of the files we've stolen from her previously and found them to be incomplete and often incomprehensible."

"At first we thought it was one of those crazy genius things," Weiss added. "Like Marshall."

"Hey," Marshall said, offended.

"But there's some kind of system," Weiss continued. "It's like a shorthand that only she can decipher."

"We think she uses it to make sure that her plans can't be stolen," Vaughn continued. "But we've made some good headway on breaking down some of the old files. While others are just impossible to decrypt."

"What about this Thirteen Stars organization?" Sydney asked. "Are they after the weapon? Do we think they know what it is?"

"Is that why they were after Sprague?" Weiss added. "Because I think killing him wouldn't be the best way to find out about it."

"But they didn't kill him," Sloane said. "They simply took out his guards. It's likely they were sending a message. I think we have to assume that Thirteen Stars wants this weapon too. It is possible that they are also going for this 'final component' and the information on the rest of the device. You will all need to take extra precautions on the mission."

"It would be helpful if we knew more about them," Sydney noted. This time she wasn't going for an implied dig. She really meant that they could use some information—*any* information—if they were expected to go up against the group.

"Jack will be looking into Thirteen Stars," Sloane said. "While the team is on board the *Triton*, he will be on a separate mission dealing with a former contact and hitting the back channels for any information on the group."

"Contact?" Sydney asked, trying hard not to raise an eyebrow. She was always interested in learning more about her father's past. Of course, that information was often a double-edged sword. So many times the things she learned turned out to be horrible surprises.

"A former associate who believes I've left intelligence work," Jack said. "See if the FBI has any information on Thirteen Stars that may have *accidentally* been left out of the information sent to the CIA."

"So we don't just have to worry about Sprague showing up, but Thirteen Stars as well," Vaughn said, summing up the mission concerns.

"There is one other concern," Sloane said.

"Of course there is," Marshall mumbled.

"Sprague is well aware of the interest in Martine and her designs throughout the world market," Sloane continued. "Not wanting to lose his investment, four of Sprague's men are with Martine and her lab at all times."

"And Martine allows that?" Nadia asked. "She didn't sound like she's the type to go along with Sprague's plans."

"Like I said," Weiss added, "she's obsessive with safety and security. It's possible she set this up. Though she seems the type to have made a separate arrangement with the guards, to make sure that what happens on the *Triton* stays on the *Triton*."

"So we have to get Martine away from the lab?" Dixon asked. "Split the guards' focus and make contact while Marshall accesses the files?"

"According to the files we have on Martine, we

know that she likes adventure," Vaughn said. "Base jumping. Sky surfing."

"Extreme ironing," Weiss joked.

"She probably booked a room on the Good Ship Lollipop so she could try out new things at every port around the world," Vaughn concluded.

"A weapons designer with a death wish," Sydney said. "How quaint."

"Exactly," Vaughn said.

"So she's probably getting bored cooped up on the ship," Sydney added. "I can't imagine that spending half a week at sea is giving her the life she's used to. We can use that to our advantage."

"She's also a bit of a player," Weiss added. "So I figure we can use that as our 'in.' Play up her adventurous side mixed with her romantic side. Now, Syd, I know you have some killer aliases, but I don't know if that will work in this instance."

Sydney picked up where Weiss left off, staring directly at Vaughn. "How do you look in a wig?"

"And a tight, revealing outfit," Weiss added. "Don't forget the tight, revealing outfit."

CHAPTER 5

LUXURY LINER *TRITON*
INTERNATIONAL WATERS OFF THE
COAST OF PERU

Sydney absentmindedly slid a piece of her blond wig back behind her right ear as she casually strolled down the hall. She had decided to reuse the wig from her mission in Bern. She was using a different identity for this mission but needed to look the same as she did in her meet with Sprague. If she were recognized, she could fall back on the Von Malkin alias and pretend that she was just trying to learn more about Sprague's mysterious weapon. It wouldn't be the first time she'd have to portray an alias within another alias, but she still hoped to avoid it nonetheless.

Even the hallways on the *Triton* were richly appointed with fine wood molding, fresh cut flowers at every intersection, and expensive artwork throughout. The only failing that Sydney could see was the bland beige color the designers had chosen to paint the ship. She figured they'd been going for soothing, but had instead managed to achieve *institutional*.

Stopping at the door to Martine's room, Sydney brushed a piece of lint off her crisp white uniform. It was the attention to detail that helped maintain an alias. The residents of the *Triton* expected the best of their crew, and Sydney knew that meant everything from knowledge of the job right down to the look of the wardrobe. A quick application of lip gloss allowed her to fire two minicameras into the ceiling before knocking on the door to Martine's four-bedroom suite.

A typical security thug dressed in a suit with smooth lines—save the bulge of a gun under his arm—answered the door. He had dark hair and a neatly trimmed beard, and his entire look was cultivated to tell Sydney that he was one of the higher-compensated members of Sprague's security force.

It figured that Sprague would only entrust his most valuable "possession" to the best.

"Yes," the man said. He looked fairly menacing, taking up nearly the entire doorway. Sydney knew that parts of the ship had been built at a smaller scale to accommodate more rooms, so it was a bit of an optical illusion that made him look so large in the smaller door. Not to say that he wasn't a large man. Just not as huge as he currently appeared.

"Oh," Sydney said, feigning surprise at the burly man's appearance. "I was looking for Ms. Stefani Martine?"

"Come in," the guard said as he let her into the living area. He was not one for small talk, apparently.

Considering the price of the suite of rooms, it was rather small. However, Sydney noted that compared to a typical cruise ship it was nearly palatial. The room had been designed with generic—though clearly expensive—furniture, probably identical to all the other four-bedroom suites on the ship. Two small couches flanked a coffee table, with another chair at the top end. The room was configured to face an entertainment center against a wall. According to the research, residents had the option of redecorating when they took possession of a suite. Obviously, Martine had decided to leave the living area as it was originally designed.

"One minute," the guard said as he moved off to a door on the side of the room. Another guard, with more of a lax and slightly disheveled look, was sitting slumped in a chair outside the door. At first Sydney had thought the man was asleep, but his eyes were open and on her. He didn't even bother to acknowledge his friend when the first guard approached the door.

The guard that had unceremoniously ushered her into the room checked back to make sure Sydney wasn't watching. Even though she was turned in to the room slightly, she was still doing her best to get a look at the keypad on the wall beside the door. But the guard shifted to block her view as he punched a security code to unlock the door. He knocked before entering what Sydney assumed was the lab. It seemed unlikely that anyone would need a security code to get into Martine's bedroom. Highly unlikely, if the report on the woman's nightly activities was to be believed.

Sydney tried to get a look into the lab, but the

big guy had managed to slip his sizeable frame through the door without providing any space for Sydney to see. It was more out of curiosity than anything else that she wanted to see the lab. She knew if everything went according to plan she'd get a full report on the lab interior at a later time.

According to the ship's blueprint, Martine had the standard four-bedroom suite. However, records also indicated that, although she had done nothing to redecorate the living room, she had had the adjoining wall between the two smaller bedrooms removed to make one large space. She also had had one of the doors blocked off. The remaining door to that large room was the one the guard had just disappeared through.

Sydney doubted the other two guards were in the lab with Martine. Weiss had mentioned that she was obsessive about security, but that would be overkill. It was doubtful the designer liked to work with anyone looking over her shoulder. Sydney assumed the guard had to punch in a code because Martine didn't like to interrupt her work to get the door herself. If there was another guard in with her, he could have simply answered the door when the other one knocked. No, the two other guards had to be elsewhere at the moment. But Sydney was fairly certain that they weren't far.

All four- and five-bedroom suites on the ship were flanked by two smaller studio apartments. The ship designer obviously took into account that anyone paying enough to buy one of the exorbitantly priced suites would bring along a staff of at least two people to be on hand at all hours of the day and night. Sydney assumed that the contingent of four guards rotated a logical two-on-two-off routine while Martine was working and sleeping. Though it was likely the configuration changed whenever the woman left the room.

Sydney couldn't imagine the room or Martine being unguarded at any time of the day or night. She was sure it made for some fairly uncomfortable visits from gentlemen if Weiss's repeated claims about Martine's sexual appetite were to be believed. At that thought, Sydney experienced a slight twinge of discomfort over how this mission was going to have to play out.

While Sydney waited in the living room, the second guard remained sitting slumped, but alert, in his chair. His eyes followed her as she moved about the room. Sydney flashed him an overly eager smile indicating that she was simply one of the ship's staff hoping to make his stay a more pleasant one.

He didn't bother to return the smile.

Sydney took a moment to case the room with an attitude that implied she was just making sure everything was to the client's satisfaction. She even ran a hand over the bar as if she were checking for dust, prepared to dress down the housekeeping staff if anything were wrong. Even with the standard-issue furniture, the room was quite impressive. She had been in lush accommodations before: mansions, castles, and even a richly appointed private plane that housed a secured computer server. This glorified stateroom was just another indulgence of the rich.

Aside from the wealth of the ship's clientele, the room told her nothing about the owner. Not a single personal memento cluttered the area. Not even a candid shot of her enjoying an afternoon above deck with her guards.

Turning her back to the guard, Sydney decided it was time to reapply her lip gloss. She pulled out the tube that Marshall had designed several years back when they were working at SD-6. The tech was always making new and interesting devices, but they found that sometimes it was easier to rely on the true and trusted creations from the past. Such was the case with the lip gloss tube containing a compressed air ejector that could launch minicameras into a ceiling. That's not to say that Marshall was resting on his laurels with his old technology. In the years since Sydney had first used the device, Marshall had figured out a way to fit four cameras into the tube. In the past he hadn't been able to get in more than three without having to remove the lip gloss and render the entire prop useless.

Sydney fired the remaining two cameras into the ceiling, faking a cough to cover any sound of impact. From the angles she had shot at, she knew one camera was focused on the lab while the other was covering the rest of the room, including the exit to the outer hall.

The door to the lab opened and Sydney turned to find Stefani Martine coming out with her guard in tow. Even in her work clothes and no makeup, the woman's file photos did not do her justice. Martine's long black hair was held back in a ponytail, which Sydney assumed was confirmation that she had been working. With her hair pulled back like that, there was nothing covering up the flawlessly smooth skin of her lightly tanned face.

Martine wore what looked like a lab coat, a green thigh-length jacket over black denim jeans and a white T-shirt. Though the outfit looked comfortably casual, Sydney could tell from the cut of the clothes and the materials that Martine was going for a very expensive version of laid-back.

The woman's long, slender body moved smoothly across the room, in contrast to the hulking lumber of the guard who had gone to retrieve her. As Martine walked toward Sydney, the guard moved off to the side. From the way he positioned himself, Sydney could not keep both guards in sight at the same time. It was a smooth move that confirmed she was dealing with professionals.

"Bonjour, Mademoiselle Martine," Sydney said as she held out her hand to the woman. English was the universal language spoken on board, but Sydney assumed that the crew traditionally greeted their guests in their native tongues.

"Hello," Martine said in response as she shook hands. "I don't believe we've met."

"No," Sydney said. "My name is Samantha Reese. I'm the new assistant cruise director."

"Ah," Martine said with a knowing smile. "Let

me guess. There is another boring mixer on the lido deck, or whatever you call it."

"It's a welcome reception in the Oceana Room," Sydney/Samantha replied.

"We've been at sea for over two days now," Martine noted. "Are we welcoming a school of dolphins that happened to swim by?"

Sydney tried to look taken aback by the woman's directness, but she wasn't exactly surprised by the question. The ship was in the middle of its yearlong round the world voyage and, as Martine noted, had left the last port of call over fifty-six hours earlier. But Sydney hadn't made up the event. She was only working with what the ship had already set up at the start of the journey.

"We are welcoming some prospective residents," Sydney explained, providing information taken from the ship's Web site.

"And your boss suggested that you should convince the reclusive Stefani Martine to attend. What do you think of that, Mr. Telasco?" she turned her attention to the big guard. It seemed everyone ignored the one in his chair. "I have been so cooped up in my room that they are now actually sending people to retrieve me."

Sydney and Martine both waited for the guard to respond. He didn't.

"Forgive him," Martine said as she turned her attention back to Sydney. "He's just upset that he's pulled babysitting duty. Mr. Telasco has a far brighter future than his boss seems to believe."

Sydney made sure she looked properly scandalized by the comment.

"Oh, I'm not his boss," Martine quickly added. "I'm just another underling."

Sydney couldn't help but think that underlings were doing well this year if her suite was any indication.

"But you probably think I'm some madwoman by now." Martine laughed. "Sorry. I've just been stuck in this room for far too long. Although I do like the idea of being the *reclusive* Stefani Martine."

"Well, the cruise director didn't call you 'reclusive,' exactly, but . . ." Sydney left off, allowing the implication to stand on its own. "She did mention that you had taken part in some of the shipboard activities when you first took up residence."

"Ah, the early days," Martine said as she stretched out on her couch. She indicated that

Samantha should sit as well, but Sydney remained standing, assuming that the staff was not allowed to get too comfortable. "I've never experienced five months go by more slowly. I fear I misjudged life on a boat."

Sydney didn't bother to correct Martine that they were on a *ship*.

"Or, more specifically," Martine continued in a darker mood, "I think someone misled me into thinking this would be much more of an adventure."

"I understand you've taken up some exciting pastimes when we've docked," Sydney said, trying to sound like a shill for the company. She wanted to get on Martine's good side but didn't want to look like she was too eager to please. She did have a role to play, after all.

"Yes, but I could fly to those destinations much more quickly than it takes to float there," Martine said. "Every day here it's the same activities . . . the same food . . . the same—"

"Men?" Sydney asked, baiting the trap. She leaned in conspiratorially so the guards wouldn't hear. She honestly didn't care if they were listening to every word—as she assumed they were—but she was going for a gossipy girlfriend relationship, and the leaning helped underscore that.

Martine stretched languidly. "You *do* understand what I'm saying. Everyone on this ship is so damned busy trying to make me happy by insisting the ship can provide everything I could ask for, they tend to forget that the ship simply can't meet all my needs. Unless there are some new services to be offered."

Sydney let the inference go without comment. "Spending all day in your room can't be very exciting," Sydney said, looking at the two guards. "Even with your traveling companions to keep you company."

"Them?" Martine laughed. "They're about as interesting as a game of shuffleboard. No. I've got my work to keep me busy."

Sydney moved in closer, deciding to sit in the chair beside Martine as if it were something a person at Samantha's level wouldn't normally do. The designer immediately perked up in anticipation of what the assistant cruise director was about to say.

"What if I told you that among these potential new residents," Sydney said, "we have a nice selection of gentlemen with a variety of interests."

"And it would be helpful to entice them with some of the single women aboard?" Martine asked.

Sydney considered acting scandalized by the suggestion, but decided against it. It was time to bond with Martine, not play the part of the assistant cruise director.

"Let's just say it could be a mutually beneficial evening," Sydney replied, feeling almost dirty at the implication.

"Well, then, I'd better lay my claim before all the good men are taken by the married women whose husbands only fly in on the weekends," Martine said with a sly smile.

"Exactly what I was thinking," Sydney said as she stood. "So then, I can expect to see you at the reception?"

"Shortly," Martine replied as she stood to show Samantha to the door. "And welcome aboard."

"Thank you," Sydney said as she left.

As the door closed behind her, Sydney chanced a glance at the ceiling, confirming that the two minicameras were still in place. She turned right and moved down the bland beige hall.

The first part of her mission was complete. Now the team was left to watch and wait while Martine hopefully got ready for the party. Any number of things could happen that would keep her from leaving the room and APO from making contact with her. Sprague could show up. Agents from Thirteen Stars could intervene. There were definite risks involved with the plan.

Sydney knew they had contingency plans in place to get to Martine in case the unexpected occurred, but she hoped that they wouldn't need to use them. It would be so much easier if they could just separate her from the guards at the party, make the offer, and get her off the ship without incident. For some reason Sydney suspected that she was pressing her luck with that hope.

Once Sydney turned the corner, she ducked into the second door she came to. It was a small studio apartment roughly the size of Martine's living room. Seeing the rest of the field team—minus Weiss—squeezed into the room was a great statement for the difference in wealth. Only the low-level rich or the servants of the extremely wealthy lived in rooms this size.

Dixon and Marshall were seated in front of a pair of laptop computers, with Vaughn and Nadia standing hunched behind them. They each had their attention focused on the screens and only glanced at Sydney as she came in.

"How's the signal?" Sydney asked as she closed the door behind her.

"Clear as a bell," Marshall said. "Though, come to think of it, how clear *is* a bell, really? Most are metal and not particularly clear at all."

Sydney didn't bother to comment on the origin of the phrase. She joined the team to check out the images. Each computer had a split screen that showed two of the angles from the four cameras she had planted. The left computer showed a pair of children running down the hall while a woman who must have been their nanny gave exasperated chase.

The computer on the right showed the split screen of Martine's living room. The woman was in midconversation with the hulking guard, while the silent one still sat slumped in his chair showing absolutely no interest in the discussion at hand.

"Maximilian should be arriving soon," the large and impeccably dressed guard said.

"Then Maxie can just wait for me," Martine said. "It was his idea to book me on this floating morgue in the first place. 'See the world,' he said. 'Think of all the exciting places you could go. The fun things you can do.' Rubbish. He just didn't want me in one place for too long for fear of someone stumbling across our little operation."

"You are an important component," the guard Telasco reminded her.

"As are you," Martine said. "And look what he's got you doing."

"I am here to do my job," Telasco replied.

"Well, forgive me if tonight I don't want to be a 'component.'" Martine said. "Now if you'll excuse me, I'm going to change." She left the room without another word.

Mr. Telasco turned to look at his sitting friend and received roughly the same reaction that Sydney had earlier, which was none at all.

"It looks like we're on now," Vaughn said as they took a break from spying. "Syd, maybe you should stay here so the crew doesn't wonder who you are. It could look a bit suspicious, if you ask me. Don't want to risk—"

"One new crew member isn't going to be noticed," Sydney said, knowing the real reason for Vaughn's suggestion. "Besides, I wouldn't miss this for the world."

CHAPTER 6

Marshall discreetly checked his pulse. It was racing. Not that he didn't already know that, but it was somehow more comforting to confirm that it wasn't just in his head. To think he had once worried about having never been outside of Southern California. A handful of missions over the previous few years hadn't prepared him for the number of times he had been out in the field since joining APO, and it was still a relatively new organization.

His heart wasn't racing just because of concerns over the mission. It was partially due to the anticipation. He was about to access Stefani Martine's secret designs. He was so looking forward to the challenge of getting into the system and finding whatever he could in her crazy coded files. No one outside of Martine knew what was in those files. He doubted that even her employer had any idea of the kinds of items she was working on. Even finding only a file on failed projects could keep Marshall busy for years simply getting into the thought process of the designer.

The woman had been responsible for some of the most intricately created weaponry the world had ever seen. One look at her CIA file was like a history on the advancement of weapons technology. Marshall would even have admitted to having a bit of a crush on her if it weren't for the fact that he was happily married. Not to mention that Martine was a murderous terrorist responsible for the deaths of thousands.

Yeah, that too, he thought belatedly.

Dixon's voice brought Marshall out of his musings. "Outrigger to team," he said into his comm. "Target is on the move."

Marshall looked at the screen and watched as Stefani Martine, dressed in a black evening gown with a plunging neckline—and an even more revealing back—left her room along with two of her guards. The lead guard was the large guy named Telasco. He nearly filled the screen as they passed the camera.

The second guard was new. From the conversation the team had picked up in the room, they knew that his name was Richard or Richards. The sound from the minicameras wasn't quite as clear as Marshall had hoped. He had already made a note to himself to get working on that once the mission was complete.

Marshall switched his attention to the screen that showed the interior of Martine's suite. Richards and an as yet unnamed buddy had entered Martine's rooms after Telasco accepted that Martine was going out for the evening. Now that Martine, Telasco, and Richards were on their way to the reception, the remaining two guards visibly relaxed in the suite. One stretched out on the couch, flipping through the menu of movie options on the in-room entertainment center, while the other was still in his position in the small seat beside the lab door. Marshall congratulated himself once again on the impressive clarity provided by the tiny cameras he had designed. The sound might have been a problem, but the video was excellent. Of course, his mind was already working on ways to improve the image quality and possibly fit five cameras in the tube of lip gloss.

"Copy that Outrigger," Vaughn replied back over the comm, bringing Marshall out of his musings. "Good luck."

"Time to go," Dixon said to Marshall as he got up and made for the door.

"Right," Marshall said. He swept a few items into his messenger bag. He was dressed casually in linen pants and a polo shirt. The shirt bore a familiar emblem on the chest to indicate he was a millionaire-playboy resident of the luxury liner. He followed Dixon out into the hall, noting that his pulse had actually jumped higher as they moved toward Martine's suite.

Dixon led the way down the hall. Once they turned the corner, they came upon a well dressed couple presumably heading for the reception in the Oceana Room.

"Pardon me," the gentleman said to Dixon. "Do you have the time? We can't seem to recall if we've crossed into a new time zone and simply missed the captain's announcement."

"Honestly," the woman said, "we hardly ever know if it's today or tomorrow on this ship."

"Well, considering we're still a distance from the international date line," Marshall said, "I would think it would be so—"

"Personally, I gave up on knowing the time days ago," Dixon interrupted with a jovial smile. Like Marshall he was dressed in comfortable casual clothes nice enough to pass for one of the jet-setting residents but discreet enough not to draw attention. "But according to my watch it's shortly after nine."

"Thank you," the couple said as they went off in the direction of the Oceana Room.

Marshall continued along the hall with Dixon. He noticed Dixon's strides had become shorter. He was clearly slowing down so they would have some extra time for the hall to clear before they reached Stefani Martine's room. Marshall looked back to confirm that the couple had turned the corner and were out of sight. He saw Dixon doing the same check on both ends of the hall before he knocked on the door.

Marshall's hand went into his jacket of its own accord. It surprised him a bit, actually, considering this was the first time on a mission he had done something like that purely on instinct. Maybe he was starting to get used to fieldwork. If everything went according to plan, he wouldn't even have to draw his tranq gun. But he found that on missions, events rarely played out as smoothly as they were expected to.

"Yes," the guard said as he opened the door.

Dixon shot the guard with his tranq gun and pushed the body inside. He managed to get the second guard from across the living room before the man could even get out of his chair. He slumped backward, as asleep as he had appeared to be since Sydney had first entered the room and placed the camera.

No matter how many times he saw the pros in action, Marshall was still in awe of what they could do. To think that Dixon had entered the room and taken out two trained guards with a minimum of fuss and muss was quite impressive. But now it was Marshall's turn to spring into action and provide some impressive moments of his own.

Marshall closed the door to the suite behind them, then hurried across the room. He was certain that Sydney and Vaughn would be able to keep Martine busy, but they still couldn't account for the possible arrival of Maximilian Sprague or any operatives from Thirteen Stars.

Stepping past the sleeping guard, Marshall unscrewed the faceplate on the security keypad and spliced open a red wire and a black one. Once the wires were connected to his handheld descrambler, it was only a matter of seconds before the screen showed him the code. Marshall punched in the ridiculously intricate number—59317486372—and listened for the lock to open. He continued to listen for any triggering devices as he turned the knob and slowly opened the door a crack.

When nothing happened, Marshall's excitement grew exponentially, as he was only a few steps away from accessing the mind of a design genius.

Marshall reluctantly stepped aside to follow protocol before entering the previously secured room. Dixon moved to the door and pushed it open carefully. His gun was at the ready in case any guards were unaccounted for. From Marshall's vantage point the room looked safe. He wanted to charge right in, but he waited for Dixon to give him the go-ahead. Considering Martine's penchant for security, they couldn't be too safe.

After a quick visual on the room from his position

in the doorway, Dixon waved Marshall forward into the inner sanctum.

The room had obviously been stripped of all the original fixtures when the two bedrooms were combined into one lab. The bland beige that ran throughout the ship's interior had been painted over with a soft white on the walls and ceiling. The carpeting had been ripped out and replaced with smooth tile. But even though the two rooms had been combined into one, it still looked like there was an invisible line down the middle separating the two sides of the lab.

On the side nearest the door was the workstation. Various tools and pieces of equipment were scattered across a worktable and various shelving units. As far as Marshall could tell, Martine employed the same organizational system that he did, that is to say, none whatsoever. Pieces of technology were scattered about the room and on the floor in the fashion of a mad genius who picked up and discarded items as needed.

The far side of the room looked as if it were under the control of the most anal person in the universe. There the crisp white of the walls and surfaces sparkled. The gray desk was pristine.

Three state-of-the-art computers sat at a workstation, softly whirring as they slept. Obviously Martine spent her time developing her ideas on that side of the room before the mad genius went to work haphazardly at the front table.

Marshall scanned the room from the doorway. Typically, the team would have scouted out the designs for the area before the mission and known they were safe to head inside. Even though they had detailed plans of the room, there had been no way to determine if Sprague's men had made alterations after the ship had set sail. They were being overly cautious in this case simply because there was no telling what a weapons designer at Martine's level could do by way of a security system.

The room seemed clean, so they were free to walk inside. Marshall watched as Dixon took a tentative step into the lab. When nothing happened, Marshall followed and went straight for what appeared to be the main computer.

Sydney wasn't the only one to notice Stefani Martine when she glided into the room. Years younger than many of the society wives, and walking with a confidence that far outshone that of the trophy girlfriends, Martine cut a swath through the party. She was in search of a good time. She had been told that one could be found that evening.

The woman was flanked by her bodyguards. Telasco stood on Martine's right. He began scanning the room for trouble the moment they walked through the door. The other guard stood on her left. He was watching the crowd but didn't seem as alert as Telasco.

It was clear that Martine was hoping to dispose of the two men accompanying her. But even at a distance Sydney could tell they had no intention of allowing Martine to stray too far. That being the case, Sydney decided it would be easier to approach Martine than wait for the woman to find her. Not that she thought Martine was looking for female companionship at the moment. At least, her file certainly hadn't indicated anything to that effect.

Sydney worked her way through the room, careful to avoid the actual cruise director, who was supposedly her—or Samantha Reese's—boss. Conveniently, certain higher-ranking members of the staff were instructed to dress up for these events so they could blend in comfortably with the passengers. Sydney was wearing a dark blue sleeveless dress, tight enough and with a slit up the leg to allow for a wide range of movement in case her evening demanded more physical exertion than a twirl around the dance floor.

All she had to do was keep the cruise director out of earshot and she could easily pass as a guest.

"Glad to see you could make it," Sydney said as she approached Martine and her guards.

"How could I pass up such an enticing offer?" Martine replied. Her eyes were scanning the room. "So now that I am here, Mademoiselle Assistant Cruise Director . . . impress me."

"Certainly," Sydney said, taking the woman by her arm and pulling her away from the guards. She didn't expect it to be that easy, and it wasn't. They followed at about four steps behind. "But first, if your gentlemen friends—"

"These are neither gentlemen," Martine interrupted, "nor my friends. And whatever suggestion you were going to make to send them on their way, you might as well save your breath. Even when they are across the room, they are right next to me. It's easier just to ignore them. They don't go away, but it's less taxing than trying to be polite."

"I see," Sydney said, playing the properly understanding hostess.

"I knew you would." Martine smiled as she clung to Sydney's arm. Sydney couldn't help liking the woman for a brief flash. Sure, she may have been strong-willed and just slightly arrogant, but it wasn't hard to imagine that being constantly under guard would do that to a person. Sydney had to remind herself that Martine would be under far tighter guard if she were sent to prison, where she belonged. Sydney held tightly to that last thought as she moved forward with the setup.

"As you can see, this event has drawn a number of our residents." Sydney grabbed a glass of champagne off a tray as a waitress passed. She was careful to grab the nearest glass and hand it off to Martine. She knew that the other two glasses had more than just champagne in them.

Sydney glanced back as the uniformed waitress— a woman in a standard *tight* servers' uniform and a red wig—offered the remaining glasses to Martine's guards. Telasco declined to drink on duty, as she assumed he would. Richards gladly accepted the drink with a flirtatious glance at the waitress. At least one of them could be expected to behave unprofessionally.

Sydney watched as Nadia continued on

through the party. She carefully weaved through the crowd, avoiding hands and making sure no one else took the remaining champagne from her. Like the glass Richards was drinking from, the one intended for Telasco had just enough of a sedative to help relax the guard into distraction, but not enough to knock him out in the middle of the party. If only both guards had decided to partake. Now Nadia would have to find another way to occupy Telasco. The guard apparently had every intention of remaining alert for the rest of the evening.

"Nothing but the same old, same old," Martine said with an exaggerated yawn. "Really, this is not what I had in mind. Where are those fresh faces you promised me?"

"Scattered about," Sydney said as she feigned looking about the room. She'd had every new passenger memorized, scoped out, and in her eyesight since she had entered the room. But she didn't want to come across as too on-the-ball for Martine. She was supposed to be the *new* assistant cruise director.

"Over there we have Señor Reyes." Sydney pointed out a handsomely elegant gentleman in his midsixties. Though the new arrival was immediately considered the most eligible bachelor on board for reasons both aesthetic and financial, she was fairly certain that Martine was looking for someone a bit closer to her age, if not a little younger. "He runs the largest banking consortium in Spain."

"Yes, I've had the pleasure of meeting Mr. Reyes through some previous business dealings," Martine said. Sydney made a note to follow up on that later. Whether Martine was referring to his financial business or her arms dealings, it was certainly worth checking out. "And while he is a perfectly fine gentleman, I am not looking to expand my portfolio. I am looking for some fun on this ship of the dull."

"How about Mr. Laslo . . . of Laslo Technologies?" Sydney jumped in as though she were truly worried about offending Martine. She pointed out a significantly overweight man two-fisting his drinks like a frat boy at a champagne kegger.

"He certainly looks like he's having a good time," Martine said skeptically. "But why do I get the feeling you're playing with me?"

"As you said, it's a long cruise," Sydney replied. "We have to find some way to have a little fun."

"Finally, a person on this boat who isn't a complete and utter bore," Martine said. "It's about time I found someone interesting to talk to."

"Excuse me, Mademoiselle Reese," an attractive young dark-haired man said as he stepped up to Sydney.

"Or someone to do other things to," Martine whispered to Sydney as she shamelessly looked the man up and down.

He was dressed in a black linen designer suit with an almost see-through gray T-shirt that hugged his torso, leaving little to the imagination. "I was wondering if you would be so kind as to introduce me to your companion?"

"I was just looking for you, Monsieur Faulke," Sydney said, feigning surprise at the interruption. "Mademoiselle Martine, please meet—"

"Taylor," Vaughn said as he took the woman's hand with his right hand and placed his left hand gently on top of it. Not as showy as a kiss on the hand, but far more intimate than a handshake. "Taylor Faulke. It is a pleasure to meet you."

Martine threw a wide smile of approval to Sydney as she replied, "And you as well. I take it you're one of the new residents."

"Still weighing my options," Vaughn said. "There is a chalet on the market in Nice that is trying to steal my attention and my bank account."

"Well, I can't speak for your bank account," Martine said, "but maybe I can keep your attention here for a while."

"You have certainly gotten off to a good start," Vaughn said as he returned the favor by eyeing her up and down.

Sydney watched, forgotten, as Vaughn took Martine off to a more private corner of the Oceana Room. The guards went to follow, though one was moving at quite a lethargic pace. Sydney watched as the two men took seats close enough to keep their eyes on Martine but far enough away to give the woman her privacy. They had obviously been through similar situations before.

Though the drugged guard seemed to be having trouble focusing, the other one kept a close watch on his subject. Sydney knew that Nadia would find a way to keep him occupied. In the meantime she kept watch on the room to make sure there were no unexpected surprises. The last thing she needed was for Maximilian Sprague to arrive. Or operatives from Thirteen Stars.

CHAPTER 7

WASHINGTON, D.C.

Jack Bristow stood at the top of the steps of the Lincoln Memorial, looking out over the frozen reflecting pool. A light dusting of snow had settled over the pool, obscuring any possible reflection. It was an odd place to meet in the middle of the night, but he was meeting with an odd person.

Jack didn't have many friends in his life. Fewer still that would be described as "quirky." He usually didn't tolerate quirky people, Marshall aside. But Marshall's quirks were countered by the value he offered in his technical genius. The man he had come out to meet proved just as valuable with other forms of information.

It was the need for information that had brought Jack to Washington, D.C., and to the feet of Abraham Lincoln. He had flown across the country for a meeting that would likely last about five minutes, simply because phones could not be trusted. Aside from the potential for tapping, a phone didn't allow Jack to look into a man's eyes or properly react to a catch in the voice. It wasn't the first time he had taken a ten-hour round-trip flight for a conversation. It wouldn't be the last.

Jack tightened his coat around him as he looked over the Mall. The white snow covered the pool and the surrounding sidewalks, dead grass, and monuments. The full moon reflecting off the snow lit the area so that Jack could see all the way to the Washington Monument. The place was empty. The homeless had been rounded up and taken indoors. It must have happened recently, because they hadn't made their way out of the restrictive shelters and back onto the frozen park benches yet.

The calm silence of the area helped Jack hear the person coming up behind him. The man was trying to be quiet, but he could do nothing about the snow crunching under his boots. Considering that only Lincoln's statue was behind Jack, the man must have been there since before Jack arrived, waiting to make sure he was alone. It was an unnecessary precaution. But Jack knew his old friend liked to play these games.

"The crow flies at midnight," a voice whispered behind his ear.

For a moment Jack came surprisingly close to laughing. He wasn't able to hold back a small smile as he responded. "And the quick brown fox jumps over the lazy dog."

"Jack Bristow," the man said as he pulled Jack around to greet him with a big hug. The use of his full name negated any attempt at secrecy in the clandestine middle-of-the-night meet. "How've you been?"

"Good, Freddie," Jack said as he managed to extricate himself from the uncomfortable embrace. "And you?"

"Can't complain," Freddie said. "And if I did, who'd listen? How's Sydney? I hear she left show business too. Still can't believe you did it. Or, more to the point, I *don't* believe you did it. But what's your little girl up to nowadays?"

"Banking," Jack said, preferring to keep his answers short. He had known Freddie Mendoza for decades. The man could extend a simple meet for hours, attempting to delve into the most intimate details of one's life. Jack found his old friend's predilection for gossip highly bothersome, but they had been through too much together to let that affect their relationship.

"And you, Jack," Freddie said, "what have you been doing to keep yourself busy? When I heard you left the Agency, I about nearly keeled over in shock. I mean, how many times did they have to arrest you before you finally called it quits? If that's in fact what you did."

Then there were times when Freddie's jovial attitude could be a considerable pain in the ass.

"Rumor has it you've been thinking of retirement," Jack said, turning the conversation around on his friend. He knew that he had to engage in a little chitchat with Freddie before he got to the point. But Jack preferred to keep the focus on any number of subjects other than his own life.

"I've been thinking of retirement since I started with the Feds," Freddie said. "Doesn't mean I'm any closer to leaving. They're going to have to pry my badge out of my cold dead hand."

Considering the man's propensity for blustering conversations and his inability for secrecy, Jack was surprised he had managed to live as long as he had. He chose not to say that, however. Freddie was easily offended when he thought anyone was making fun of him. Not that Jack ever made fun of anyone.

Jack listened for a few more minutes as Freddie rambled on about his own family, his work at the FBI, and the general incompetence of the government as he saw it. Jack had heard it all before. No matter what administration was in charge, Freddie's rant rarely changed. The whole conversation was pointless, but Jack's return flight didn't leave for a few more hours, so it wasn't like he had anywhere else to be at the moment.

But Jack's tolerance for idle conversation lasted only for so long.

"Of course, we're not meeting out here in the middle of the night to talk about the next State of the Union," Freddie said as his tone shifted from jovial to serious. Conveniently, he knew how far to take his banter and when it was time to get down to business. It was one of the main reasons Jack stayed in touch with the man over the years. That and the fact that he was a tremendously useful source of information.

For decades it had been a joke how little the CIA and FBI trusted each other. The CIA was charged with protecting the United States from foreign enemies. The FBI's purview was restricted to crimes committed within the borders. Naturally, these areas of responsibility overlapped from time to time. Stories about the lengths to which each agency had gone to withhold information from the other were often shared over drinks in whispered, though lighthearted, conversations in D.C. bars.

Recent historical events had brought the issue into a more serious light. Some people had gotten it into their heads that the intelligence community should behave as a *community* and learn to play well with each other. As with anything else related to the government, the CIA and FBI were slow to come around. The agencies still kept secrets from each other, but now the whispered conversations were no longer lighthearted.

Before the current PR bonanza forced the agencies to at least *appear* to work together, CIA and FBI agents on the lower rungs had had to find ways to share information without catching hell from their superiors. As such, contacts were made between agencies on a more personal level— friendships that existed solely for the purpose of sharing information necessary for getting the job done. At times these secret relationships between agencies caused problems—when information flowed a little too freely, but for the most part they served their purpose in helping curb illegal actives around the world and within the borders of the United States.

"I'm interested in a terrorist group working in the U.S.," Jack said. "Thirteen Stars?"

"Terrorist group?" Freddie said. "Don't think they'd agree with you on that title."

"I doubt there are many terrorists who would," Jack said.

"'Course you'd have to ask them yourself," Freddie rambled on. "Shouldn't be too much of a problem for a man like you to get a meet and greet."

"Until that time," Jack said, "what would the members of Thirteen Stars consider themselves?"

"American heroes," Freddie said. "Walk with me and I'll fill you in." He started down the steps of the Lincoln Memorial and headed in the direction of the Vietnam Veterans Memorial, more commonly known as the Wall.

"Most terrorists consider themselves heroes," Jack said as he followed. "Or martyrs."

"Or both," Freddie agreed. "And when you get down to it, Thirteen Stars are the same as any other group."

"They haven't seemed very successful," Jack said, remembering all the failed assassination attempts they had made over recent years.

"And how does a man measure success, exactly?" Freddie asked. "Some would say they've been pretty persuasive in the way they've been getting their message across. But tell me, how do you know what they've been up to?"

"I've seen some files," Jack said. He knew he was saying more than he should, but that was the only way he was going to get more information out of Freddie.

"And exactly whose files have you been looking at?" Freddie asked, knowing it was a fairly loaded question. "Just exactly who are you working for these days, Jack? Retired CIA officers don't usually go around checking up on unauthorized organizations working on American soil."

Jack remained silent, as was his preference in these situations. He was willing to go only so far in trading information.

"Shutting down on me again, huh?" Freddie said. "Can't count the number of times that's happened over the years. Just tell me one thing, Jack."

Jack could tell by the tone in Freddie's voice that the playfulness had come to an end.

"Tell me I should be sharing this information with you."

Jack chose his words carefully, as he *always* did. "I am the same man with the same responsibilities you have always known."

Freddie considered Jack's words for a moment. Then he smiled and continued walking. "'Course you are. Just had to hear it. You know as well as anyone, it's not that easy to go around sharing classified information."

"Understood."

"So these files you've been looking at," Freddie said, "they're not all that informative, are they?"

"Which is why I've come all this way in the middle of the night," Jack said.

"And here I thought it was so you could catch

the late set at the Red Velvet," Freddie joked. "But about those files. Don't think you know the whole story. Thirteen Stars has been a mite more successful with some assassination *attempts* than you may think. It's just certain people have it in their interest to keep that out of the files."

"I don't suppose you'd care to tell me what people?"

"Nope. Not at all," Freddie said. "But I do have another question for you. Have you noticed any similarities between the targets of Thirteen Stars?"

"As you've pointed out, it's not entirely clear what actions Thirteen Stars has been involved in since their formation," Jack said. "From what I've learned, they are suspected in a range of activities involving a diverse set of victims from criminals to dignitaries."

"And how often has there been a difference between the two?" Freddie asked.

"True, the more 'distinguished' names on the list have been known to operate outside of the law."

"And that's the cause of Thirteen Stars in a nutshell," Freddie said as the reached the Wall.

Jack noticed that someone had already come

by to clear snow from the listing of the names of the fallen. Since the walkways around it were still covered, Jack assumed that whoever had been by had done so recently. Probably long after dark and long after the grounds crew had gone home.

"What is their ideology?" Jack asked. "What motivates them?"

"Truth. Justice. All that bunk." Freddie laughed, sending out tendrils of smoke from his breath in the cold night air. "They kind of go in where the government can't. Or won't. They see themselves as true Americans, fighting for life, liberty, and the pursuit of evildoers the world over. But they want to go about it honestly. None of this cloak-and-dagger we all seem to be engaged in nowadays. Can't tell the good guys from the bad and all that."

"It's always been that way," Jack said, knowing how the words were especially true coming from him.

"Well, maybe it has, maybe it hasn't," Freddie said. "Either way, Thirteen Stars has had enough. And they've been working quietly over the years to take care of those criminal-types the government isn't dealing with for one reason or another."

"And the FBI isn't concerned about this?" Jack asked.

"Oh, we're *concerned*, all right," Freddie said. "Damn concerned. But there's just so much we can do about it. They're good. They go in, get the job done, and get out. No muss. No fuss. And they're not glory hounds about it either."

"That last part may have changed," Jack said as he slipped his hand into his coat pocket and pulled out the business card Sydney had found in Bern.

"What's this?" Freddie asked as he looked over the card. "Interesting."

"I take it you've never seen this before?" Jack asked.

"Nope. Nice logo. Cuts right to the chase," Freddie said. "Where'd you find it?"

"Let's just say it was left behind on purpose," Jack said. "Do you think it's from Thirteen Stars or someone trying to out them?"

"Could be either," Freddie said. "Or neither. Could be a coincidence altogether."

"And how many coincidences do you find in our line of work?"

Freddie put his hand on Jack's shoulder warmly.

And Jack allowed it. "If this card *does* belong to Thirteen Stars, it means they don't want to be in the background anymore. They're looking to make a name for themselves now. And *that* is a bit of a concern."

The words hung in the air for a moment.

"Mind if I hold on to this?" Freddie asked as he tried to slip the card into his pocket.

Jack intercepted the man's hand and retrieved the card smoothly. "Sorry, but I may need it. When you get home, don't be surprised if you find a copy of the image in your e-mail."

"Won't be surprised at all," Freddie said as he stepped away from Jack. "Well, it was good seeing you, Jack. Now I'll be leaving before you can ask the million-dollar question."

"Freddie," Jack said in a warning tone that stopped the man.

"I think we've covered just about everything," Freddie said.

"You still haven't told me who they are," Jack said. "Who's behind Thirteen Stars?"

"Well now, Jack, there's classified, and then there's *classified*," Freddie said. "I'm afraid I can't share that particular information with you.

Considering I don't know who you're working for, your word only goes so far. Mind you, it goes further than most, but there are some things I'm not ready to share. Let me just say that Thirteen Stars may be a little closer to home than you might think."

"So—"

"Sorry, Jack," Freddie said, extending his hand. "I've said all that I can. And all that I will. Information doesn't go quite as far now as it did in the old days. You know, with the whole new spirit of cooperation and all that."

"Thank you," Jack said as he took the man's hand. "I appreciate what you've given me."

"Only for you, Jack. Only for you."

"Now you should get home to your lovely wife," Jack said. He even managed to squeeze out a forced smile.

"'Lovely' my ass," Freddie said. "Why, you know what that woman . . ."

It took another five minutes before Jack could extricate himself from the conversation. Honestly, he didn't mind. If he had, he never would have mentioned Freddie's "lovely wife" in the first place.

The two parted company at around one fifteen. Jack's flight was still a few hours off, so he decided to take a short excursion to a late-night jazz club that Freddie had mentioned. The Red Velvet was far enough off the radar that he knew he wouldn't run into any of the D.C. elite or, worse, any tourists. He settled in at a table with a brandy and thought over the mysterious Thirteen Stars while a light-skinned African-American woman with a deep melodic voice sang of summertime.

The members of Thirteen Stars obviously saw themselves as revolutionaries, given the choice of their name. It should have been clear to Jack from the start. Every group in the world has a cause based on some strict sense of morality as defined by the membership. The real problem began when they started forcing the group's version of morality on others.

Working in secret allowed Thirteen Stars to right the wrongs as they saw fit, and—as Freddie proved—with little interference from the government. Now that it looked as though they were going public with their activities and leaving behind quite literal calling cards, Jack expected their operations would escalate.

Jack's cell phone began to vibrate in his pocket. He quickly stood, leaving his drink behind, and slipped out the back door to take the call. Aside from suspecting that he needed to be in private, he had no intention of disrespecting the singer with his call.

Any number of people could be calling him in the middle of the night, but he was surprised to see the number that had come up on the screen. It was a number he had called only a few hours ago, belonging to a person he had just left.

"Freddie?" Jack said as he picked up the call.

"What can I say," Freddie's voice said over the secure connection. "I miss you already."

"Is something wrong?" Jack asked.

"Not really," Freddie replied. "At least, not so far as I can tell. But I thought you should know, this calling card image you sent me . . . Well, I forwarded it along to the night crew, and . . . Where did you say you got this card?"

Jack knew that he hadn't given that particular detail. He weighed the options on sharing the information. It took only a few seconds. Ultimately Jack decided that Freddie had called for a reason. It was likely that he wasn't about to share anything until he got something from Jack.

"From a third party," Jack lied, since that wasn't the important part. "Someone who picked it up following an assassination attempt on an arms dealer by the name of Maximilian Sprague."

"Well now, isn't that interesting?" Freddie said. "It seems that another one of these cards popped up earlier today. Looks like Thirteen Stars *is* ready to start making a name for themselves."

"The card?" Jack said, trying not to sound impatient. "Where was it found?"

"Next to the body of Maximilian Sprague," Freddie replied. "Looks like someone went back and finished the job."

CHAPTER 8

LUXURY LINER *TRITON*
INTERNATIONAL WATERS OFF THE
COAST OF PERU

Marshall stopped before he reached Martine's computer. He knew that they were on a tight time schedule, but something on the worktable drew his attention. It was a metal arm about a foot long and Y-shaped. Nothing about the component looked especially interesting, except that it was on the one part of the table not overrun with junk.

He wanted to touch it. To pick it up and examine it. There was something about the way it sat on a makeshift pedestal separating it from the jumble of other electronics and tools. It was almost as if the metal piece had been given a position of honor. The tools she used with it were shined and carefully laid out on a velvet cloth, while the other tools were haphazardly spread throughout the room.

This piece had something to do with the mysterious device that Sprague had been talking about. That much was clear. But what Marshall still didn't know was what it was being used for. He leaned in to get a closer look and noticed that the metal arm was attached to two wires that led under the table. It was rigged to an alarm, making it all the more interesting.

"Marshall, we don't have much time," Dixon said softly but urgently as he checked the screen on his PDA.

Marshall couldn't see what Dixon was looking at, but he could easily figure it out. The PDA was linked in to the video from the minicameras Sydney had placed in the living-room and hall ceilings. Since the door between the living room and lab was open, Marshall assumed that Dixon was keeping an eye on the hall. The rest of the team would warn them if Martine or her guards headed back to the room, but they still needed to be prepared for the unexpected. The last thing they needed was for Sprague to show up while Marshall was elbow-deep in Martine's computer.

Marshall tore himself away from the interesting piece of equipment and continued past the piles of metal and wires to the clean side of the room. He could sense a slight rise in temperature as he neared the computers. Martine must have been working on something for a while before she left for the party. The rest of the room was kept several degrees cooler than normal room temperature, probably for the sake of the computer hard drives.

Once Marshall roused the sleeping system and began playing around in it, he wasn't surprised to find it had several layers of security that he would need to get through before he could get into the files. Even if she hadn't had a penchant for security, a genius like Stefani Martine wouldn't just leave her work lying open for any teenage hacker to get into. Of course, Marshall had surpassed most teenage hackers back in the third grade.

"This is going to be fun," Marshall said as he plugged his computer decryption device into the computer's USB port. Though he would have preferred the challenge of a solo hack, he knew they didn't have time for him to do things by hand. Working in conjunction with the machine, he was able to run code-word and number searches electronically.

Stefani Martine wasn't the type of person who would have her code word written on a piece of paper taped behind a picture. Her code would be a series of meaningless letters and numbers in a seemingly random order that secretly meant something to her. Much like the code to get into the lab. It was likely that she would rotate that series of digits monthly. Marshall was a little disappointed that it took only a minute for his handheld hacker to reach the right combination.

"Oh, we're kickin' it old school," Marshall said as he saw the second line of defense. "I love a good riddle."

The computer's second security protocol was a series of questions like those asked on some financial Web sites, the kind run by people who think it would be easier to remember the answer to a generic question than a code word that was a combination of your children's names and birth dates. There were twenty-five questions on the list, but Marshall hardly bothered to look them over. There was secure, and then there was insane.

Someone with Martine's stunning mind needed access to the computer when inspiration struck. Those kinds of intense geniuses didn't have the patience to type in twenty-five answers and wait as each one was submitted for approval. There was another clue to this pass code. It was something Marshall's hacking device would not be able to figure out.

Luckily, Martine had grown up around the world. One of the three colleges she had attended was in the United States. Though she always returned to her native homeland of France, she had clearly adopted English as her primary language. Marshall was glad to see that he could read all of the questions. He doubted he would have had time to translate them all from French.

"Time to go Indiana Jones on your hard drive," Marshall said as he scanned down the list of clues. Twenty-five questions ranging from the basic "What is your mother's maiden name?" all the way up to the extremely personal "What was the name of your first love?"

For a moment Marshall rethought his initial

belief about Martine's level of patience. According to everything he had read in the mission brief, she was obscenely secure with her information. But another quick run down the list provided the answer he was looking for. He had his answer, and he only needed to know the one.

It was the same basic logic that was taught in high school when preparing students for the SATs. When presented with a series of answers, start out by eliminating the obvious and go from there. In this case it was the obvious that would be his answer. The one code he needed was the answer to a simple question.

True or False: Maximilian Sprague is an *abruti*.

It was the only question that asked for an opinion. It was the only question that had a French word in it. And it was also the only one in a True or False format.

Marshall wasn't sure what an *abruti* was, but he assumed it wasn't nice. He took hold of the optical mouse, clicked on "True," and held his breath as the screen went blank. A moment later a prompt popped up asking for another password.

"Sweet!" Marshall said as he set his hacker to work again. This time he was in the system in under thirty seconds. "And here we go." Marshall removed the decryption device and replaced it with the transmitter. The plan was to uplink the files directly to APO through an orbiting satellite so the techs back home could start going through the files immediately.

"Merlin to Starman," Marshall said as he switched on his communications link to APO headquarters.

"This is Starman," came the eager reply from the voice of Drew Tennet. He was the youngest member of Marshall's team and—at only twenty-two—the one that seemed to have the most promising future in tech. Sure, he didn't have close to Marshall's abilities, but you could only expect so much from an underling.

Normally the person being contacted at APO headquarters wouldn't have a mission code name. Drew certainly wasn't going out in the field anytime soon. But he had asked—well, *begged*—Marshall to let him have a code name of his own, since he would be the contact for the mission. Marshall had tried to explain that it wasn't quite the way things were done, but after watching Drew's face droop, Marshall had immediately relented.

Marshall wasn't good at dealing with disappointment from his direct reports. Carrie was always telling him that he needed to be a stronger boss, but she had the added benefit of being a far stronger person than he would ever be. And so, Drew Tennet had become Starman.

Of course, it took a while to get the *right* code name. Drew had started with his handle Spikeiscool4774. Marshall had had to point out that the name was a bit cumbersome to say, especially in the event of an emergency. Then Drew had tried Dark Phoenix, which Marshall had to nix because it might get confused with Sydney's code name. Starman was the eighth name Drew had submitted for approval. It wasn't great as far as Marshall was concerned, but it wasn't problematic, so they'd gone with it.

"I'm sending through the files," Marshall said. "I need you to—"

"I know what to do," Drew replied succinctly. Marshall knew he had a tendency to micromanage, but that was no excuse for the kid to be so abrupt. Marshall figured that Sloane was probably standing over the poor guy's shoulder. He decided to cut Drew some slack for the moment. If it continued, though, Flinkman might have to have a little talk with his staff when he returned.

"Accessing," Marshall said.

As the files uplinked, Marshall scanned through the pages on the hard drive. The information being transmitted was moving at a rate too fast for the human eye to see, but that didn't stop Marshall from scrolling through the file names on his own to see if there was anything interesting.

Since he could personally absorb information as fast as a computer from the seventies, Marshall quickly skimmed through the files one by one. Each file was named after a literary or mythological reference. As Weiss had warned, the actual files themselves were a jumble of shorthand information, but Marshall knew enough of Martine's system to get the gist of each weapon.

He went through all the files, committing the subjects to memory before moving on to the next. He was moving rapidly. Not just because of their time constraints but because he knew Drew was also seeing the screen as Marshall saw it, and he wanted to test the kid to see if he could keep up.

He was moving so quickly that he almost missed the importance of a file named "Sword of Gaia."

"What was that?" Marshall asked, having already opened the next file.

"What was what?" Drew asked, confirming that Marshall was still the fastest draw in the West.

He clicked out of the file and went back to "Sword of Gaia." Upon reopening the file, his fears were immediately confirmed. He looked over to the worktable where the Y-shaped metal arm was resting, and shivered.

"Oh, dear," Marshall said in an amazing understatement.

As the same screen flashed up at APO, Drew said something far more appropriate for the situation, had he not been sitting in front of Mr. Sloane at the time.

"Marshall, what have you found?" Sloane asked over the comm, ignoring Drew's outburst.

"You know that special project Maximilian Sprague told Syd about? This is the most . . . I mean it's . . ."

"Spit it out, Marshall," Sloane scolded over the comm.

"Sorry . . . It's—"

But before Marshall could say what it was, it started to go away.

The words began to jumble on the screen. Entire lines of text scattered and changed into symbols and then nonsense.

"No. No. No. No. No," Marshall repeated as his hands flew over the keyboards. "Drew, what did you do?"

"Nothing!" Drew replied, and Marshall could hear the quick tapping of keys over the comm. "It's got to be a security virus."

It *was* a virus. And it was moving faster than any that Marshall had ever seen. But it wasn't just destroying Martine's files.

"It's accessing APO's systems," Drew cried frantically. "It's trying to break in."

"I know!" Marshall said through clenched teeth. He had given up trying to save Martine's files. Now he was just focused on keeping the virus from destroying APO's computer infrastructure. With every door he closed, another two were opened. His fingers couldn't move faster than the computer, even with Drew working just as frenetically on the other side.

His only hope was a manual disconnect. He hated to do it, but there was no choice.

Marshall ripped the cable out of the USB port, severing the satellite connection.

"Did we get it?" he asked over the comm.

All he heard back was the tapping of keys.

"Drew!"

"We stopped it," Drew replied, and Marshall could hear the relief in his voice. "I think we're okay."

It wasn't a definitive answer, but it would have to do for now. Even if Drew had been 100-percent certain, Marshall knew he wouldn't be satisfied until he got back into the office himself and could tear the system apart for a full diagnostic. Until then he would have to request that everyone limit the computer use.

"Were we able to save anything?" Sloane asked.

"I don't know," Drew replied. "What do you think, Marshall?"

But this time Marshall didn't reply. He was too busy working the keys on Martine's computer.

"What is it, Marshall?" Sloane asked. "Can you get back through the security system?"

Marshall shook his head as if Sloane could see him. He then looked up at Dixon, without bothering to mask the concern on his face. "The virus wasn't part of Martine's security system. It was . . . something else."

". . . *mais, il n'y avait personne à bord du bateau*," Vaughn said, lamenting the fact that Taylor hadn't met any interesting people on the boat. He followed it up with a sip from the nonalcoholic champagne Nadia had given him. It wouldn't do for him to actually get drunk while getting Martine tipsy.

"*Quel voulez-vous?*" Martine replied before switching to English as if she no longer cared who heard her. "This boat is full of bored people who live bored lives and think it will be more exciting by simply adding water."

"You seem to be regretting the decision to live here," Vaughn said.

"I was," Martine replied. "Until now." She ran her hand through his jet-black wig. It felt odd having her play with his hair that wasn't really his. He honestly hadn't needed the wig, but Sydney had insisted on it. He knew that she had only been playing with him, but he figured it didn't hurt to go along with it. Besides, he knew he'd never hear the end of it from Weiss if he weren't "man enough" to wear the wig.

It was nice to know that Sydney was forced to wear one as well on this mission. Not that she hadn't worn more than her fair share over the course of her lifetime.

Vaughn was a little uncomfortable when Martine's hand continued sliding through his hair and down the side of his face, and came to a stop on his chest. He felt bad for using this woman, until he reminded himself that her crimes were far worse than a not-so-innocent flirtation. But it was still odd to know that every move he made on this woman was being watched by Sydney, Nadia, and at least one guard.

Vaughn suddenly gained a deeper appreciation for all the times Sydney had had to feign intimacy while any number of people—including her father—watched or listened in. On the other hand he was also far too familiar with how Sydney must be feeling right now, watching the act.

"I am still not sold on purchasing one of these *salles d'apparats*," Vaughn said in character. "They all seem so *petite* for the amount."

"Unlike a chalet in Nice," Martine suggested.

"The truth of the matter is," Vaughn said, "I was looking for some excitement. But no matter how far I go from home, France always pulls me back."

"There is no other place like it in the world," Martine agreed.

"And tempting as you may be," Vaughn said, "you are not exactly selling me on the idea of living aboard this ship."

"*Oui*," Martine admitted, throwing a wave in Sydney's direction. "Sammy over there would be very disappointed in me. I don't believe I'm quite the salesgirl that she was hoping for."

"I didn't realize you and Ms. Reese were so close," Vaughn said with a raised eyebrow. "Maybe she'd like to join us?"

"Watch it," Sydney's voice whispered in his ear. He had almost forgotten she could hear every word he was saying.

"She's on the staff," Martine said dismissively. "It's her job to make sure you're happy here."

"Well, then she is doing it quite well," Vaughn said as he stroked Martine's hand with his. "Because I am very happy at the moment. And as for the ship, I can see there are some benefits."

"Now do not assume that I am one of those benefits, Monsieur Faulke," Martine said. She coyly slid her hand away from him and took a sip of her very real champagne.

"Not at all," Vaughn said as he scanned the room. Sydney had moved from his line of sight, but he knew she was watching and listening. "I was referring to the financial benefits of living like this."

Looking left, Vaughn could see that one of Martine's guards was fighting to keep his eyes open. Considering how little sedative Nadia had put in the guards' drinks, it was likely the guy was a lightweight. The sedative on top of the single glass of champagne had obviously been too much for his delicate system.

The other guard, Telasco, was at heightened alert. Nadia was working overtime to keep him distracted. It seemed to be working, thanks to the skimpy outfits the servers were squeezed into.

As a backup Nadia had brought the big guy a glass of water, which Vaughn assumed was also laced with a sedative. Though it was in Telasco's hand, he had yet to sip from it, as far as Vaughn could tell. But that wasn't a problem at the moment, since Vaughn noticed the guard's other hand was resting on Nadia's thigh.

"Financial. Yes, those are the only benefits," Martine said. "Although opportunities like *this* do come along once in a rare while."

"Opportunities like this?" Vaughn playfully asked as he leaned into her. At that precise moment he caught Sydney watching him. He almost wished he hadn't, for what was about to happen.

"Opportunities like you," Martine said as she moved forward and their lips met.

Vaughn closed his eyes so that he couldn't watch Sydney as he played into the passion. Martine was a practiced kisser. Strong yet gentle on the lips. He could see how she had gained her reputation.

"I hope you're taking notes," Sydney's voice whispered in his ear. Vaughn tried not to laugh.

After the requisite time had passed, he broke the kiss and pulled away slightly.

"I'm not sure how I feel about such a public display," Vaughn said. "Especially in front of people who could very soon be my neighbors."

"These people are so full of their own lives, they don't care about what two consenting adults do in front of them."

"But do they care about what two consenting adults do in the privacy of their own rooms?" Vaughn asked.

Martine smiled through her champagne haze. "Would you like to find out?"

"It would be my pleasure," Vaughn said as he stood.

"*Oui*," Martine replied as she rose and took his hand. "It most certainly will."

Vaughn glanced behind him to see that Richards' attention was presently focused on the floor three feet in front of him. And Nadia's body was blocking Telasco's view. It seemed likely that the guy was more focused on the hand that had risen slightly up Nadia's thigh. If it went any farther, it was likely Nadia would be causing a different kind of distraction soon.

Sydney nodded, acknowledging that they would move on to the second stage of their plan. She would stay behind for a moment to make sure Vaughn and Martine got clear of the Oceana Room without incident. If Telasco decided to go after Martine, Sydney had a needle full of sedative that would stop him.

Vaughn wasn't sure exactly what the protocol

was when Martine went off with one of her suitors. Maybe this was the kind of thing the guards tended to turn a blind eye to. Martine certainly hadn't been thinking about her escorts when she decided to sneak off with him.

Once Sydney knew they had gotten away safely, she would sneak out to join him in making the offer to Martine.

Martine clung tightly to Vaughn as they stumbled through the reception. She could not have been nearly as drunk as she pretended to be on a glass and a half of champagne. Vaughn assumed this was part of the game she liked to play with her suitors. The innocent damsel who would turn into a predator once they were alone.

There truly had been some very interesting reading in the file that Weiss had showed him earlier. But Vaughn really had no interest in finding out what Martine was really like when alone. Aside from the fact that he had a mission to carry out, his heart belonged solely to another.

And she would be along at any moment.

Vaughn escorted Martine out of the Oceana Room without attracting much attention, other than that of the single men and women who seemed to be lamenting the fact that the two of them were no longer available. But more important, no guards followed. There were no shouts of alarm. Just a man and a woman going off to do whatever people would do in these situations.

They strolled arm in arm to the stateroom Vaughn—or Taylor Faulke—was looking to purchase. Of course, there was no actual room. The plan was to tease her with a stroll on the deck first. There he would make the government's offer. It was too dangerous to go all the way back to the studio apartment where they had set up shop earlier. Aside from being too close to Martine's apartment, it was in the opposite direction from their extraction point.

"You seem to be in a hurry," Martine said as they quickened their pace.

"Can you blame me?" Vaughn replied.

It was hard to think of this woman as one of the world's foremost authorities on weaponry that could be—and had been—used to destroy nations. Then again, it was just as strange to know that the woman he truly loved could kill him with one well-placed punch.

Vaughn's thoughts were still on Sydney when

he and Martine turned a corner and he was struck by a well-placed punch of a different kind. He wasn't even able to see who had thrown the punch because everything suddenly went dark.

"We need to leave," Marshall said. "Now."

Dixon knew better than to ask questions. Marshall was excitable, but professional. If he said they had to leave, they had to leave.

Dixon pulled his gun and moved to exit the lab, stopping in the doorway to confirm the living room was still empty except for the sleeping guards. No one had approached the cameras in the outer hall, but he knew from years of experience that there was always another way into any room. When he looked back he was surprised to find that Marshall wasn't behind him. The tech was looking over the Y-shaped metal arm sitting on the worktable.

"Marshall, I thought—"

"One second," Marshall said as he carefully lifted the device off its pedestal. It seemed to be attached by a pair of wires. "We can't leave without this."

"What is it?" Dixon asked. "Marshall, what's going on?"

"Just a second," Marshall replied as he traced the wires to a small box under the table.

"Outrigger to Phoenix," Dixon said into his comm. "Something's up. We may need to abort."

"Keep me posted," Sydney responded. He could hear the tension in her voice. It reflected the tension in his own.

"Hand me those wire cutters," Marshall said, pointing to the tool lying atop a pile on the shelf by Dixon's head.

Dixon kept one eye on the doorway as he reached for the wire cutters. He was forced to holster his gun for a moment so he could keep the PDA out while he handed the tool to Marshall. Once that was done, he took the gun out and went back to his position in the doorway.

"Um . . . you might want to wait outside while I do this," Marshall said with an almost imperceptible quiver in his voice.

Dixon had no intention of leaving his partner. He felt helpless as he glanced back to watch Marshall clip one wire, quickly followed by the other. Marshall paused as if waiting for something to happen. When nothing did, he got off the floor, grabbed the device, and made for the door.

"Fifty/fifty chance," Marshall said, causing Dixon to realize just how much of a risk they had just taken.

"Now can you tell me what's going on?" Dixon asked as they moved through the living room.

"The virus wasn't a security system," Marshall said as they reached the door leading to the outer hall. "Someone hacked into the ship's wireless system, broke through Martine's firewall, and accessed her computer."

"Wait," Dixon said before Marshall could open the door. "To do that—"

"The hacker has to be on the ship." Marshall concluded the sentence.

"Outrigger to Phoenix. We have an unknown third party on board," Dixon said into the comm.

"Get to Martine now and meet at the extraction point."

Sydney's response was quick and concise. "Copy."

Dixon knew that Sydney would complete the mission. Probably by taking Martine against her will. Then Sydney would escape with the rest of the team. His objective was to get off this ship with Marshall and the apparently essential piece of technology.

"I assume that's something we're going to need?" Dixon asked, nodding toward the device.

"Someone's going to," Marshall said. "But I don't think we want them to get it."

"Stay behind me," Dixon said as he moved in front of the door.

"No worries there," Marshall replied.

Dixon checked the PDA one last time. The hall within range of the cameras was empty. But that didn't mean that it was clear around the corners or behind any one of the doors around them. If someone was hacking into the wireless system, they could easily be nearby. He slipped the PDA in his pocket and placed his free hand on the doorknob with his gun at the ready. Dixon opened the door and stealthily stepped into the hall. Once he had a visual confirmation that the path was clear, he motioned for Marshall to come out.

Dixon led Marshall down the hall, heading for the extraction point. The original plan had them stopping back in their room to pick up the equipment they had used earlier. Dixon didn't want to risk that because it was in the opposite direction, and it was likely someone was already on the way to Martine's lab to get the device in Marshall's hand. The laptops had already been wiped of information and fingerprints. When someone stumbled across them later, there would be no evidence linking them to APO.

"Maybe Sprague was the person accessing the system," Marshall suggested.

"Not likely," Dixon said. "The files ultimately belong to him."

"Maybe he found out we were in the system," Marshall said. "Didn't want us to get the files."

"If he knew we were in the system, we'd be dead," Dixon said. "No reason to infect the computer and give us time to escape."

"So we're thinking it's the same people who shot at Syd in Switzerland? Thirteen Stars?"

"Let's hold off on worrying about the identity of the third party until we get whatever it is you're carrying safely off the ship," Dixon said.

"Good point. We could spend all night going over the list of enemies of the state," Marshall said as they turned a corner and came upon a tall blond woman holding a gun on them. "Or we could just ask her."

Dixon raised his gun automatically. He didn't want to risk a shoot-out in the middle of the ship, but not knowing his enemy made any negotiations nearly impossible. He may not have known her motives, but he had a fairly good idea what she wanted. They were not about to hand over their only bargaining chip. Not that he understood what it was.

"Give me the device," the woman said by way of introduction.

"Sorry," Dixon said, "I don't think it belongs to you."

"Funny," the woman said, "somehow I doubt it's yours, either. Don't look like an attractive French woman to me." Her accent was distinctly American. It sounded like there was a slight Southern drawl to it, as if she had tried to train it out of her but it wouldn't quite die. That could be faked, but Dixon failed to come up with a reason why she would go to the trouble.

"You know what they say about possession and the law," Dixon replied.

"Well, honey," the woman said, "I don't care about the law. But we'll have to do something about that possession."

With a swift and sudden move the woman kicked Dixon's gun out of his hand. Instinctively he managed to grab her leg on the upswing and send her flying onto her back, forcing her to lose her own gun.

"Go!" he said to Marshall, pushing him back in the other direction. It was a longer route to the extraction point, but it was safer than trying to get past the woman on the floor.

Once he saw Marshall on his way, Dixon turned back in time to take a fist to the jaw. The pain was sharp but not blinding. Her fists continued to come at him in rapid succession. At first all he could do was block. Once he saw an opening, he sent a body blow that knocked the wind from her.

The woman's gun was sitting on the floor between them. Dixon lunged for it, but the woman dropped to the floor and swept his legs out from under him. Dixon rolled back, kicking the gun away from her in the process. If he couldn't have it, he was damned if he was going to let her get it.

Dixon came out of his roll a few steps away from his own gun. Not wanting to let her out of his sight, he backed toward the gun, but she threw herself at him before he could reach it.

Dixon used the woman's momentum to carry her up and over his body as he fell on top of his gun and sent her flying behind him.

The gun slammed into Dixon's shoulder as he hit the ground. He saw bright pinpoints of light as a wave of pain and nausea washed over him.

The woman was on top of him in an instant, pummeling his face with her fists. Dixon tried to buck her off him, but his legs were locked in place under her knees. He pulled at her arms to defend against her blows, but she managed to get a few past. The woman was a well trained professional, even reminding him a bit of Sydney. He knew that the only way out of this was to take her by surprise.

As he continued to block her punches, Dixon's eyes flitted to the sides of the hall, looking for an escape. Nothing was there. His body continued to shift as they fought, and he could feel the gun slide out from under his back. It was unlikely that it would go off as it worked its way out, but the odds of that weren't entirely in his favor.

Using all his strength, Dixon tried to roll the woman off him. He only succeeded in freeing the gun, which the woman quickly snatched up.

"Where did your friend go?" she asked as she held the gun in his face.

"It's going to be hard to find out that information if you shoot me," Dixon said calmly. If he were going to get out of this, he could really use that element of surprise about now. To gain the upper hand, he'd need to conserve his energy and make his move when she least expected it. Dixon closed his eyes and slowed his breathing to relax himself.

"Hey, we're having a conversation here," the woman said, slapping his face. "Don't be rude."

Dixon reopened his eyes and was glad to see that the element of surprise had actually come to him instead of the other way around.

Marshall was standing over them.

"I said, where is your friend?"

"Right here," Marshall said as he slammed Martine's metal device into the woman's head.

• • •

"Copy," Sydney said abruptly as she signaled Nadia to make for the exit. She knew her sister would follow once she had a chance to get away.

Sydney assumed Dixon meant that operatives from Thirteen Stars were on the ship. The identity of the third party didn't really matter at the moment. It just meant they needed to speed things up. Vaughn was supposed to have warmed Martine up to their offer before Sydney arrived to play bad cop. It looked like the bad cop was just going to show up a little earlier than expected.

As Sydney reached the entryway, she glanced back to see that Nadia was having a difficult time keeping Telasco's attention. The initial flirtation seemed to have passed. His hand was no longer resting on her thigh. Both hands had her by the arms as he tried to gently push Nadia out of his line of sight.

But Nadia wasn't giving up so easily. Staying completely in character, she managed to keep the guard at bay, giving Sydney at least a few more minutes before he realized that Martine was out of the room.

Richards, the drugged guard, was less of a concern. His head had lolled to the side, indicating that his attention was far from the location of Stefani Martine at the moment.

Sydney pushed her way past the party latecomers and in the direction of the bank of elevators that would take her to the upper deck. Nadia would give her a couple minutes to get away, then head for the extraction point herself. Of the team, Nadia was the least at risk of being discovered. As long as no one tested the drinks she had mixed with sedatives, she was in the clear. Nobody ever noticed the serving staff.

Outside the Oceana Room the halls were empty, which was much easier for Sydney than having to continue to push her way past people. She tried to convince herself that everything was fine, despite Dixon's warning. Sydney walked at a brisk pace, not wanting to call too much attention to herself.

Not knowing what was happening at the moment, her body was screaming at her to run, but she knew that could just as easily alert the unknown third party to their location. It was a big ship. They could manage to take Martine in very easily, so long as they didn't cause a scene.

Sydney turned a corner and froze. The plan had suddenly changed. A group of well dressed passengers were bunched up down the hall. They were looking at something on the floor. She couldn't make out what it was that had captured their attention, but her heart sank with the assumption.

Considering that something interesting was already happening in that particular hall, Sydney risked breaking into a run to cover the distance between her and the commotion. Her fears were heightened when someone said "Call the ship's doctor" and Sydney saw a familiar black suit lying between the well dressed legs.

Sydney pushed through the crowd and confirmed what she already knew.

Vaughn was on the ground. He was breathing, but not moving.

"I'm a member of the crew," she told the people around her. "I'll take care of him. No need to worry. You should get back to the party."

"Are you sure, dear?" an older woman asked, a look of serious concern on her face. "Someone should go for help."

"Already taken care of." Sydney smiled, trying to will the crowd away. She pulled her earpiece out to show them. "I've sent a message over the crew communication system."

"Isn't that something," the woman said, in awe of the miniature device. Sydney knew she shouldn't go around showing CIA technology, but it was only an earbud, not some piece of classified equipment. There were far more pressing concerns at the moment.

"Oh, Rachel, you should see what we're doing with cellular technology at the lab," the woman's gentleman companion said. "We'll all have personal phones that size within the next five years."

In the midst of the chaos, Sydney couldn't help but think that Weiss would want her to get him the name of the company for his stock portfolio. Naturally, she had no intention of stopping the man to ask. It was just one of those weird things that pop into the head when the brain is on overload. With Vaughn unconscious, Martine missing, and members of Thirteen Stars possibly on board, it was somehow suddenly perfectly logical for Sydney to be thinking about stock tips.

The group of partygoers had apparently lost interest in the commotion and were heading back toward the Oceana Room. The conversation had already moved away from the unconscious man on the floor to the crazy new things they could do with technology these days. The attention span of the idle rich never failed to surprise Sydney.

"Come on, Vaughn, wake up," Sydney said as she lightly slapped his face. "Where's Martine?"

His eyes flitted open, then shut again. He was regaining consciousness, but very slowly.

"Vaughn," she pleaded.

"Samantha!" Nadia's voice called from down the hall. "Mr. Telasco would like to speak with you."

Sydney looked up when she heard her sister call her by her alias. The still lucid, still huge guard was barreling toward her. Nadia was closing in on the guy, with Richards lagging considerably behind in his drug-induced haze. Sydney laid Vaughn's head back on the floor and sprung up between him and the guard.

"Where is Stefani?" the guard demanded as he approached her.

"I'm afraid I don't know, sir," Sydney said innocently. "I came to look for her myself and found Mr. Faulke on the ground unconscious. You don't think there's been a mugging on the ship? This is horrible. It's only my first week."

The guard looked as if he were going to go with

the story. Then he grabbed Sydney and slammed her against the wall.

"Where is Stefani?" he asked through clenched teeth.

"Get off her," Nadia said as she grabbed his arm and pulled him off her sister.

Richards managed to catch up at that moment. He apparently found a reserve batch of clarity and hooked himself on to Nadia's free arm. He wasn't exactly a huge concern, but the other guard used that moment to lash out at Nadia, sending her and his partner flailing to the ground.

Sydney used the distraction to free herself. She pushed the guard back and sent a kick to his chest that slammed him into the opposite wall.

The guard jumped back at her, attempting to slam her into the wall again, but Sydney ducked out of the way as he hit the bland beige paint job. As he smacked wall, Sydney sent her elbow back into his spine. She had hardly made contact when he spun, hooked on to her arm, and sent her back to the opposite wall.

As Telasco approached her again, Sydney swung her leg forward, kicking him in the stomach and then kneeing him in the face when he doubled over. She slid her hand under her dress, grabbing for the syringe strapped to her thigh beside her gun. As the man fell to his knees, Sydney stabbed him in the neck with the needle and injected him with the sedative. He was out in seconds.

In the meantime Nadia had easily managed to get the upper hand on the drugged guard. As she was about to land a final blow, Richards fell over of his own accord. The combination of sedative, champagne, and exertion had apparently done him in.

"Syd," Vaughn said as he roused himself. "Someone got Martine."

"Do you know where they went?" Sydney asked as she knelt beside him.

"I didn't see," he replied.

Sydney looked at Nadia. "Well, they didn't go back to the party. So they must have gone toward the elevators or the Promenade. Put the guards in that storage closet"—she pointed to the door halfway down the hall—"then take Vaughn to the extraction point. I'll go after Martine."

"Alone?" Nadia asked.

"Dixon and Marshall are probably with Weiss already," she said. "It will take too long for them to get back."

Nadia looked down at Vaughn. It was clear that she didn't want to separate from Sydney, but there was little choice.

"Be careful," Nadia said as she knelt beside Vaughn and gently helped him up.

"I'll be right behind you," Sydney said as she took off down the hall.

Not knowing exactly where to go or what to expect, Sydney cautiously rushed toward the Promenade. If the kidnapper had taken Martine into the elevators, they could be anywhere on the ship at this point. The Promenade was the only chance to find the woman. The residential luxury liner was considerably larger than the average cruise ship. And there was no guarantee that Stefani Martine and her kidnapper were even still on board.

"Phoenix, come in."

It was just what she didn't need at that moment. Arvin Sloane's voice was suddenly in her ear.

"Go ahead," she said into the comm as she moved through the halls.

"Outrigger and Merlin made contact with an unidentified woman," Sloane said. "They escaped, but she's still on board, so be careful."

ALIAS

"She's not alone," Sydney said. "Someone has Martine. I'm not sure if it was Sprague or someone else."

"Sprague is dead," Sloane reported. "It was Thirteen Stars."

"Then I'd say the odds are that they're here now," Sydney said.

"Be careful," Sloane said in that fatherly tone that drove her insane.

"Phoenix out," she said, putting an end to the conversation.

Sydney carefully continued on her way as the hall turned left, then right, and left again. It finally opened up onto the ship's two-story shopping district known fittingly as the Promenade.

At this hour most of the upscale shops were closed, but there were still some stores that remained open twenty-four hours, ranging from high-end convenience stores to an all night coffee shop. The Promenade was the town center for this city on the sea and was still quite busy with those not interested in the partying going on in the Oceana Room.

Sydney froze when she heard the excited murmuring and realized the crowd on both the upper and lower levels was focused on one spot in the middle of the first floor of the Promenade. Sydney pushed her way through the people, sure of what she was going to find. She would have preferred to not make a scene, but one had already been made for her.

Once she reached the center of the throng, she saw the ship's paramedics working on Stefani Martine. Sydney had seen enough death in her work to know they were just making a show for the passengers. The woman was long past resuscitation. The two bullets in her chest had seen to that.

CHAPTER 10

"Everyone please give the paramedics room to work," Sydney said to the crowd in an official tone. Posing as a crewmember had been effective so far. She figured the paramedics wouldn't question it if she continued. They probably even appreciated the help.

"Is there anything I can do?" Sydney asked one of the men as she knelt beside the body.

"There's nothing anyone can do," he replied.

Sydney nodded her head gravely as she stood up and moved back into the crowd. She had expected an answer along those lines, but that really wasn't why she had bent down to ask it in the first place. The move had allowed her a closer inspection of the body. It had already rewarded her with her first clue.

Sydney paused for a moment as the medics wrapped up their work.

Martine was dead, and Sydney wasn't quite sure how she felt about it. On the one hand, the death would put an end to the horrific weapons of murder the woman routinely created for profit. On the other hand, she was a person. A complex person, actually. Of course, Sydney really hadn't had the chance to get to know her, but she could tell that outside of their professional lives she and Martine would have gotten along. Then again, considering that so much of Sydney's world revolved around her professional life, she wasn't exactly sure what she was outside of it. But that was a personal discovery for another time.

The killer could still be here, Sydney thought as she scanned the crowd, looking for anyone out of place. The Promenade was packed with people and more were coming in. Apparently, word was spreading quickly, aided, no doubt, by the story of the unconscious man who had been found outside the Oceana Room. The entire ship would probably be abuzz soon enough.

As she looked over the people, Sydney listened to the clips of conversations for clues. There were plenty to be found.

". . . just shot her right in front of me."

". . . he didn't even care that we were here . . ."

". . . cameras must have recorded it . . ."

The pieces of conversation confirmed what Sydney suspected. The only reason to kill someone so publicly was *because* the killer wanted the death to be public. A shooting in the middle of a street in Switzerland. A death in the middle of a cruise ship's mall. These weren't just murders, they were messages. But messages to whom?

"Ma'am, you should step back as well," a security guard told Sydney.

"Sorry," she replied as she slipped back out of the crowd. She had gotten what she needed, though she hadn't had the chance to look at it yet. It had been lying beside the body. Sydney assumed it had fallen out of Martine's hand when the paramedics made their show of attempting to resuscitate her. Sydney didn't have the chance to look at it until she cleared the growing crowd, but she already knew what it was. It was the second one she had seen that week.

The black paper card was an exact duplicate of the one she had found in Switzerland. The white star in the middle also contained the number thirteen written in black. The discovery confirmed that Thirteen Stars was behind both attacks, which wasn't a surprise. But it did beg the larger question.

Why is Thirteen Stars so focused on publicity all of the sudden? Sydney wondered.

Sydney looked up from the card and continued her scan of the sprawling Promenade. A man was staring down at her from the second floor. Even at that distance Sydney could tell that he wasn't looking down at the commotion. Or the dead body. He was looking at *her*. She was glad that she had gone with the blond wig, because he seemed to be trying to memorize her features.

Sydney didn't want to give him the time to stare, but she wanted to get a good look at him as well. She knew the moment she moved he would run. She made a visual imprint of his salt-and-pepper hair, his darkly tanned skin, and his well conditioned body. The man didn't seem to mind that she was looking.

But eventually he decided that enough was enough, and he turned to leave.

Sydney knew that he wanted her to give chase. He would have slipped away quietly before she had noticed him if that wasn't the case. No. He had been waiting for her. He wanted her to follow. And as much as she didn't want to play into his hands, Sydney knew she couldn't just let him get away.

Since no one else on the Promenade was paying any attention to her at the moment, Sydney gave up any pretense of stealth and went after the man. She took the stairs two at a time as she rushed to the second floor, past the closed shops, and down the hall. The climate-controlled air that kept the ship's interior at perfect room temperature seemed to be getting cooler as she ran.

He was leading her out to the ship's top deck.

Sydney burst through a pair of still swinging double doors, scaring a man out for a late-night stroll under the starry sky. It wasn't the man she was chasing, so Sydney apologized as she brushed past him, continuing the hunt. Once she focused her attention on the deck, she didn't have to worry about tracking the man. He was dead center in the spotlight of a helicopter hovering overhead.

The few other people on deck were visibly confused by the night landing. It didn't help that the
helipad was on the other end of the ship. She
couldn't believe that anyone would be crazy
enough to land on the relatively thin slip of deck
between the ship's outer walls and the rail.

If Sydney was even the least bit still concerned
about attracting attention, the helicopter was taking care of that for her. A murder followed by an
unscheduled landing would have the ship's entire
security force on them in moments. If Sydney was
going to get any answers, she needed to stop the
unidentified man immediately.

A chain-ladder dropped from the helicopter,
derailing any concerns over a landing. Sydney
launched herself at the man as he reached for the
bottom rung. The impact of body against body
knocked him away from the ladder and sent them
both sprawling to the polished wood deck.

Even though Sydney had taken him by surprise,
the man recovered quickly and was first back on
his feet. Up close he looked to be in his early fifties
and in incredible shape. But Sydney didn't have
time for any more observations. The man kicked at
Sydney as she tried to stand, but she ducked out of

the way. Her momentum took her into a backward roll that brought her back to her feet.

They faced off as the helicopter continued to hover. The rotors were blowing the cold sea air around them, and Sydney was having trouble staying on her feet. She was also having trouble keeping her wig on her head. Eventually she had to give in to the wind as it whipped the wig off and sent it flying over the side of the ship, allowing her actual hair to fall down around her shoulders.

The man reacted visibly when Sydney's disguise fell away. There seemed to be a moment of recognition, or it could have just been surprise at realizing that she wasn't someone he had accidentally stumbled across. She had been here for a reason, just as he had.

The pair circled each other looking for an opening. Sydney still had her gun strapped to her thigh, but she preferred to take the man in without resorting to shots. There were too many variables to try to take him out safely on the deck as a crowd gathered to watch. She didn't want to risk killing him either. Sloane would want to know why Sprague and Martine were murdered. He'd also want someone to punish for interfering with his plan.

The man swung first, but Sydney jumped back and he met only empty air. As he completed the swing, Sydney kicked him, sending her heel into his side. But he rounded back on her, with an elbow to her raised knee.

A shot came from the helicopter above. She almost didn't hear it over the sound of the rotors, but she saw wood kick up from the deck at her feet. She needed cover, but she couldn't let the man get away. She spotted a safe harbor only a few yards away but needed to position the man that way.

Another shot was fired as Sydney moved left so she was beside the man as he stood along the ship's rail. She threw her body at him, pushing the man's almost immobile mass back several feet. He grabbed her arm and then flipped her up and over him. Sydney used the momentum to twist her body in the air and come down on her feet. It wasn't easy to do in heels, but she stayed upright and had managed to get where she wanted to be: a few feet away from an upturned lifeboat strapped to the side of the ship.

The lifeboat placement was more decorative than functional, but that didn't matter to Sydney. As she slid back under the cover that it provided, she could hear another bullet rip into the edge of the lifeboat. She was safely out of the helicopter's line of sight.

The move had surprised her opponent for a moment, but he recovered well. The man grabbed the edge of the upturned lifeboat hanging above him and swung at Sydney with both feet. Knowing she couldn't jump out from under the cover of the lifeboat, she braced herself as best she could. The impact still sent her crashing down to the deck on her back.

The man was on her in seconds. Sydney tried to get away, but he grabbed her by the neck as she tried to get to her feet. He was choking her. Sydney could feel her larynx constricting. She tried to gasp for air, but nothing came. The smack into the deck had already knocked the wind out of her. She didn't have much in reserve.

Sydney looked into the man's eyes. He didn't have hate in them. He did not have fear. If anything, he seemed to look on her with pity.

Whatever his motivation, she was not going down this easily.

Sydney slid her legs beneath her, doing her best to slip into a crouch. Getting up onto the balls of her feet, she threw all of her strength into her legs. Pushing up, she launched herself into the man. He released his grip as he fell back into the rail. She watched the pain register in his face as his spine connected with the rail.

In the moment Sydney took to get her breath, the man scurried out from under the lifeboat and climbed the rail. He grabbed the chain-ladder, and the helicopter pulled him up into the air. Sydney grabbed after him, but only came back with a handful of the cool night air.

In the light from the helicopter, Sydney could see the man was smiling. But he wasn't simply relishing the victory. There was something else in the smile. A look of added triumph.

As he pulled farther away, Sydney watched him mouth the words "See you soon."

She could only watch as the spotlight went out and the helicopter flew off in the distance. Not only were Martine and Sprague dead but their killer had escaped. This was not a good day.

"Hold it right there," a voice from behind Sydney said.

And it wasn't getting any better.

Sydney turned to find five men in security

uniforms with their guns trained on her. Each of the men seemed to be at a different level of comfort with holding a gun on a woman.

"You're going to need to come with us," the guard closest to her said. He seemed to be the one in charge. He even had a fake metal badge that said CHIEF on it. It looked more like a child's toy than an actual uniform piece.

Sydney imagined that, cheap uniforms aside, the men were all properly trained. The ship's residents would have demanded the best. The amount of wealth floating beneath their feet was almost unimaginable. Still, the guards probably never honestly expected to deal with the kind of night she was having. Probably had to deal with nothing more than a few neighborly disputes. They could have grown soft. Either way, they were just doing their jobs and Sydney had no intention of hurting them.

She had no intention of going with them either.

"It's okay," Sydney lied as she backed away from them. "I don't want to cause any trouble."

Sydney stumbled as she backed up. Her hand slid down the side of her tight-fitting dress. "Sorry." She smiled. "I think I broke my heel." Sydney bent as if she were about to pull off her shoe. Instead she reached under the slit in her dress and pulled out the gun strapped to her thigh.

The guards didn't even have time to register what she had done, before Sydney was armed. She was aiming her gun at the security chief.

"Now, I'm truly sorry," she said calmly. Affecting a casual attitude was the best way to keep the guards from realizing that even with her gun they still far outnumbered her. "But I really have to be going."

"Ma'am," the chief said. "We're in the middle of the Pacific. And I don't see any helicopters coming for you right now."

"True," Sydney said as she took a few steps to the right. The guards kept their eyes trained on her the entire time. "But a helicopter escape's already been done. I have something much more exciting planned."

"Oh, do you now?" the guard played along. "And you wouldn't care to tell us your little plan, would you, missy?"

Sydney reconsidered her take on killing the condescending jerk, but decided to play along instead. "A professional never gives away her secrets. But I will tell you, I plan to start with this—" Sydney fired her gun. The bullet whizzed above the head of the security guard and took out the winch above him. The mechanism split in two, releasing the rope that held the lifeboat. It came crashing down on the guards, trapping them under the heavy wood.

"Sorry once again," Sydney shouted through the boat bottom as she ran. It wouldn't take long for the guards to extract themselves, and more security was certainly en route.

Passengers moved out of the way but still managed to stare at the well dressed woman running the deck in heels. Sydney knew the ship was large but hadn't realized just how big it was until she was running all the way from the bow to the stern.

She passed a deck sign as she ran. Somehow she found it fitting that this was called the sports deck. She was getting more than enough exercise on it for one night. She just hoped it wasn't going to be any more hazardous to her health than it had already been.

She heard the shot before she saw the bullet flick into the rail beside her. Security had caught up to her surprisingly quickly.

"Stop right there!" a new voice yelled behind her.

Sydney didn't bother to look back or slow down. There were enough civilians out on the track-like deck that she knew security wouldn't risk firing more shots. She weaved through people who were bending and ducking out of the way of the bullets she knew would not come.

Sydney slipped out of her shoes so she could run more easily. She needed to increase her lead on security if she was going to get away clean. She was almost at the aft rail. It wasn't like she was running out of boat, but she had no intention of running in circles all night. She was coming up on her exciting escape, as she had told the guards.

The lockbox was several yards ahead of her. She could see that the lock was sitting on the ground beside it, confirming that at least one of the team had already been here. Sydney chanced a glance back as she reached the box. Almost a dozen guards—including the ones she had left at the bow—were after her.

Sydney reached into the box and pulled her escape route out. With another quick glance at her pursuers, Sydney got up and continued toward the stern. She slung the coil of rope over her left shoulder and reattached the gun to her right thigh.

The rail was only a few yards away.

Sydney took the grapple at the end of the rope and hooked it on to the rail. She dropped the rope over the side and grabbed on to the decelerator. Taking one last look back at the approaching guards, she jumped over the side.

The cool ocean air breezed past her as she dropped past deck after deck, falling fourteen stories until she landed square in the center of the waiting boat. Even she was impressed that she had hit the target so directly, and attributed the perfect landing to the impressive ability of the captain.

"Weiss's Water Taxi at your service," Eric Weiss said from his spot behind the wheel. As soon as he saw she was on board, Weiss pulled the boat out of the ship's wake and headed out to sea.

Sydney looked over the deck of the small yacht and saw Dixon and Marshall examining some piece of metal equipment. Marshall kept smacking Dixon's hand away, even though it was nowhere near the device. Nadia was trying to tend to Vaughn with a cold compress to his eye, but he was already up and moving to Sydney. She could see a bruise had already formed, but it wasn't quite a black eye.

He grabbed a blanket off the deck chair and

wrapped it around her, keeping his arms on her for comfort and warmth. Now that she had finally stopped moving, she realized just how cold it was on the water. But it felt nice under the blanket and in Vaughn's arms.

True, the mission had been a failure, but she looked over the team and saw that none was the worse for wear. She took comfort in the fact that at least they had all gotten out of it relatively unscathed.

LOS ANGELES

"Hi, honey. How are my two favorite people?" Marshall said into his cell phone as he walked through the crowded airport terminal. He could hear Mitchell laughing in the background as he spoke with his wife, Carrie. "Sounds like somebody's having a good time."

"Well, actually, *somebody's* laughing because he thinks his breakfast looks funnier on me than it does sitting in the bowl," Carrie replied tensely. Marshall tried not to laugh too, remembering what she had looked like the last time her hair was full

177

of soggy Cheerios. "And after I get off the phone *somebody* is going to be having a time-out!"

Even though it wasn't directed at him, the threat immediately sobered Marshall's mood. He remembered all too well the time-out *he* had gotten when he laughed at her the last time this happened.

"Please tell me you're at the airport," Carrie said pleadingly into the phone.

"Well, I'm at *an* airport," Marshall replied as he bypassed the luggage area since he had no checked bags.

"Marshall."

"I'm sorry, honey," he replied as he stepped outside into the brilliant L.A. sunshine. "I'm still in Chicago. I kind of missed my flight. Crazy security screeners. Just because I used one of my suitcases from . . . my old job . . . as a carry-on. I mean, how was I to know it had a small amount of explosives residue still on it?"

"Oh, Marshall," Carrie said, sounding more exasperated than concerned.

"It's okay," he replied. "Everything worked out fine. Just missed my flight . . . and the next one."

"I thought we were going to see more of you

with your new job," Carrie said. "How much travel does the bank's IT department really need to do."

"I know, I know," he said. He *hated* lying to Carrie, but if she knew what he did for a living, she would understand why he needed to lie. Although if she *did* know, he wouldn't need to lie anymore, so that made the whole line of thought pointless. "It's just the conference. I learned all about this cutting-edge—"

"So when will you be home?" Carrie cut him off. Although she had always loved talking to him about the technology he had created back when they were working together at the Joint Task Force on Intelligence, she was easily bored by his supposed new job when he spoke about the exciting world of financial systems.

"Tonight?" Marshall said as a question, since he really didn't know for sure. He braced for an explosion as he quickly made an offer. "But I swear, I'll watch Mitchell all weekend. You and the girls can have a spa day or poker night or whatever it is you do when you get together."

"I think an impromptu trip to Vegas is a great idea," Carrie said eagerly. It was clear she wasn't misinterpreting him. She was just changing the plan. He couldn't blame her. He was leaving her alone with Mitchell far more often than he liked. It made sense that she would get frustrated from time to time.

"I'll call Pam and Cathy," she continued, sounding much happier. "See you when you get home."

"I love you," he said.

"Love you, too," Carrie replied as she hung up.

Marshall couldn't help but think that she hadn't sounded all that upset about missing him once the Vegas trip came up. He knew she was just punishing him. Not that he deserved it. It wasn't his fault he needed to get to APO immediately to run a diagnostic on the entire computer network and perform a proper scan on the metal device tucked safely into his carry-on.

Sydney shot him a look of concern as he closed his cell phone. All Marshall could do was shrug. He was just doing the best that he could, like any working parent.

He said his good-byes to the rest of the team as they split into the three sedans. Everyone else was going home for a quick change before reporting in, but Marshall didn't have that luxury. He was needed in the office immediately.

It totally bummed him out that he couldn't even start his day with a quick visit with his son. But he knew he had the important job at the moment. Identifying that metal arm and seeing if anything could be salvaged from Martine's encrypted files took precedence over everything else. Especially if the weapon Sprague had been teasing Sydney with was really what Marshall thought it was.

As the driver took him through the streets of Los Angeles, Marshall pulled the Y-shaped device out of the bag. He hadn't wanted to risk taking it out during the commercial flight with other people around, but he couldn't stand waiting another minute without examining it. Considering the driver was with APO, it was safe to take a look at it in the car.

The metal arm looked no different from the last time he'd seen it. Smooth gray metal slightly over one foot long, three inches wide, and two inches thick. It was heavy, meaning that there were more than just wires inside. At each of the two ends of the top of the *Y* there were female connectors, meaning it plugged into something. And three wires sticking out of the base indicated that it was probably a part of something bigger. If he had read them right, Martine's files seemed to indicate what the item was, but Marshall didn't want to think about that until he had proof.

Traffic on the 10 freeway was surprisingly light for the time of day, so it only took a little over a half hour to get to the train station that housed the secret offices of APO. Because he was alone, Marshall figured it would be okay to just ride in the car to the station directly. The others would probably take a subway car from another station when they came in later, so it didn't look as suspicious.

The driver left Marshall off at the station's drop-off area. Before heading inside, Marshall grabbed a coffee and a Danish, since there was no food service on the plane and he was starving. Then he went down to the station and into work just like any other businessperson.

Of course, his commute from the station to the office was considerably shorter than most.

As usual, Marshall's eyes needed to make the adjustment from the dark train tracks to the bright white offices of APO. Conveniently, there was a short entry hall that made the transition a little easier on the eyes. Once inside he made a brief pit stop to report in to Mr. Sloane, and then headed for his workshop.

"Do you have it? Did you bring it?" Drew Tennet asked as he scurried toward his boss, before Marshall had even reached his office. The kid was practically shaking with anticipation.

"Wow, *Mitchell* isn't even this excited to see me when I come home from a trip," Marshall said. "By the way, I didn't bring you anything."

"Very funny," Drew said.

"How are you doing with the network?" Marshall asked. He was enjoying teasing the kid by holding off on showing him the goods. Any proper tech geek would be floored by the device.

"Eighty-six percent secure," Drew replied as they moved into Marshall's office. "I don't think we lost anything. And I doubt anything got in."

"Cool," Marshall said. He'd been expecting to have maybe 50 to 55 percent of the computer secured when he came in. Drew was truly exceeding all expectations. "Um . . . did you . . . go home last night? Or sleep? At all?"

"Well, I did nod off somewhere around five this morning," Drew said. "But only for a few—maybe five—minutes."

"You haven't been, like, downing the coffee, have you?" Marshall asked. Since the kid was absolutely bouncing off the walls, it was a logical question, and Marshall felt suddenly odd about the coffee he was holding in his hand.

"Mountain Dew, baby," Drew said. "The nectar of the tech gods."

Marshall remembered well the days he'd spent in college downing nothing but that particular elixir.

"Okay, well, I'm . . . Don't let Mr. Sloane hear you referring to your superiors as 'baby,' and . . . Well, just start there," Marshall said as he opened his bag.

"Sure thing, dude," Drew replied.

Marshall just shook his head as he removed the device from his bag.

"Wow," Drew said, for no apparent reason. It was just a metal piece of equipment. There was nothing special about it except for what it possibly connected to. But Marshall understood the excitement. It was the anticipation of just what the device could do that was exciting and frightening at the same time.

"Any luck reconstructing Martine's files?" Marshall asked as Drew looked over the metal arm.

"Some," Drew said, preoccupied with the technology. "But not enough. I've been focused on the Sword of Gaia file but have zilch to show for it."

"Let me see what you got," Marshall said as they went over to Drew's workstation. After Drew woke the sleeping laptop computer—which had probably gotten more rest in the previous few minutes than Drew had all night—Marshall dug into the files.

As Marshall suspected, Drew was downplaying his success. The kid was more than halfway to decrypting the fragged file. But as with any good tech, for Drew anything short of a complete success was a failure. And Drew was a good tech.

But now it's time for Flinkman to shine, Marshall thought.

"Good job, Drew," Marshall said, recalling a talk Sydney had given him about praising underlings. "I can totally build off this."

Marshall could sense the Dew-fueled smile of Mountain Drew as he worked on the computer. Drew had already laid some impressive groundwork. Clearly much of Martine's files were forever beyond recognition, but the key file, which the kid had spent all of his time on, was definitely promising. And when Marshall added his touch to the mix, he managed to rebuild the entire file in under fifteen minutes.

The top line info on the file had only a basic encryption. That was the same in all of Martine's files.

It was an ego thing. She wanted any interlopers to know what she was working on, but she wanted to restrict access to the actual technical specs. Even then, all of her files were incomplete. She kept half the information for every project in her computer and the other half in her impressive brain. That way no one could ever access an entire file and steal her designs.

No matter how hard Marshall worked to decrypt the file, he knew it would not contain everything he needed to know. That didn't really matter, though. Just the idea of what Martine had been working on was enough.

"Oh, dear," he said again, repeating his reaction from the *Triton*. Even though he had already guessed what the file referred to, it was still overwhelming to see it in front of him. When he turned the laptop toward Drew, the kid also had the same profanity-laced reaction he'd had earlier.

Once again Marshall thought to himself that it wasn't entirely appropriate and made a mental note for a future conversation about acceptable language for the office.

"What do we do now?" Drew asked.

"We tell Mr. Sloane," Marshall said as he saved the file and closed the laptop.

"We?" Drew asked as the sugar from his last drink fully kicked in.

"I couldn't have gotten this without you, kiddo. You deserve the credit," Marshall said as he started to leave. "Just . . . don't say anything while we're in his office . . . or *ever* speak in Mr. Sloane's presence. That's a good rule of thumb too."

"'Kay."

Before they left for Sloane's office they stopped to pick up the metal arm from Marshall's desk. Marshall was already having second thoughts about bringing the kid along. It wasn't as though Drew had never spoken to Mr. Sloane before. He *had been* the point person while Marshall was away on this mission. But this discussion was more than just an update. It was a far more important briefing than Marshall had thought he'd be having in reference to this mission.

"Um . . . Mr. Sloane," Marshall said as he knocked on the door frame to his boss's office. Sloane was talking quietly with Jack Bristow. Marshall hated to interrupt but knew that he had to. "Hi, Mr. Bristow. How was D.C.?"

"Fine."

"I'm glad you're here too," Marshall said as he

came into the room with Drew. "You know Drew, right? Drew Tennet?"

"We've met," Jack said in the manner he tended to use when he wanted Marshall to hurry along.

"Right, well, we've found something," Marshall said as he put the laptop on Sloane's desk. "Something in Stefani Martine's files."

"What is it, Marshall?" Sloane asked as he sat up in his chair.

"It's . . . well . . . this," Marshall said while opening the laptop. The screen popped up on the Sword of Gaia file. "It's a seismic bomb. Actually, it's the seismic bomb to end all seismic bombs. The most powerful one ever created."

"We're talking *Superman* seismic," Drew added. "And no flying around the world to reverse time is going to bring back the coast when it drops into the ocean."

"Okay, um . . . Drew is being a little overzealous," Marshall said, shooting the kid a look. "I'm pretty sure we're talking seismic *not* cataclysmic."

"Right now neither of us is exactly sure *what* you are talking about," Jack said. "Can you please start from the beginning?"

"Sure," Marshall said as he scrolled through

the file to show the first image. It was an archival photo of a huge old seismic bomb. "In the beginning there was a bang. A really *big* bang. Sorry. Couldn't resist. Anyway. Back in Vietnam and Korea, American bombers used what was known as a seismic bomb. Now, this baby weighed fifteen *thousand* pounds and packed quite a wallop. It destroyed everything on the ground within a three-hundred-meter radius. But the crazy part was, everything within a radius of three kilometers would shake, rattle, and roll with the aftershock."

"Thank you for the history lesson, Marshall," Sloane said. "But what does this have to do with Stefani Martine? As you said, the technology for seismic bombs has been around for decades. What was she doing with it?"

"This," Marshall said as he called up the designs on Martine's device. It was considerably smaller than the original seismic bomb. Rather than needing to be dropped from a plane, it could be stored in a small crate. Maybe even a large trunk. "Ten times the power. One quarter the size."

Sloane leaned in to get a better look at the device. "Are you saying—"

"That you dig a hole and drop this bomb into

the ground around a fault line, you're going to get one heck of a wake-up call," Marshall said. "The actual bomb blast is inconsequential compared to the damage the ensuing quake would cause."

"How much destruction?" Jack asked.

Marshall shot a look at Drew. "It would be bad. We're not talking about California-falling-into-the-ocean bad—well . . . probably not. . . . It's all kind of theoretical at this point. But it would cause some serious destruction."

"Imagine it," Drew said, unable to stay quiet any longer. "You put this thing in a third-world country that doesn't have the quake retrofitting of, say, Los Angeles and you could probably wipe out a civilization."

"Again," Marshall added tersely, "we don't want to be alarmists, but it could get ugly."

"And what is this thing?" Jack asked as he reached for the metal arm.

"Best I can tell," Marshall said, "it's the heart of the bomb. Martine was very careful with the device. She created the outer casing first. That's the part that actually directs the blast outward to start the shaking. This . . . This is the core itself. The thing that sets it all off."

Jack carefully laid the device back on the table.

"Don't worry, it's not functional," Marshall said as he grabbed the device. "As far as I can tell. I mean, if it were, it probably would have gone off when I clocked that woman with it to save Dixon." He couldn't help but notice that Drew took a couple steps away from him.

"Where is the outer casing?" Sloane asked.

"Beats us," Drew said. "We haven't accessed that part of the file."

"Best I can tell, Martine's notes indicate that she shipped it off to a storage facility while she worked on the core," Marshall explained. "She was careful not to have the two pieces near each other in case they fell into the wrong hands."

"But Thirteen Stars already has the files, correct?" Jack asked. "The complete, undamaged files."

"Well, with Stefani Martine there's no such thing as *complete* files," Marshall said. "But yeah, Thirteen Stars has the files without the messy virus attached."

"So we have to assume they are on their way to getting the outer casing," Sloane said. "And what will stop them from creating their own version of the core?"

"There's nothing in the file that would tell them how to construct it," Marshall said.

"Far as we can tell," Drew eagerly added.

"Yes," Marshall said, shooting the kid a warning glare. "But it makes sense. Martine was very careful to make sure no one but she could build this thing. As long as we have the core and Thirteen Stars has the casing and *no one* has the complete file on how to build it—which probably died with Martine . . . Well, then the bomb remains useless to everyone."

"But just in case," Sloane said, "get back to the files and see if you can come up with a location on the casing. It would be better if we had both components under our control."

Marshall couldn't help but notice the suspicious look that Jack shot Sloane. Marshall almost shuddered when he considered what the old Sloane could do with such a device. He felt worse when he realized that once upon a time he, Marshall, would have been expected to recreate the device for SD-6. If this kind of technology had existed back in the day, Marshall could very easily have helped destroy a nation. Luckily, that was all in the past. He didn't work for *that* Sloane anymore.

This is the new, improved Sloane Version 2.0, Marshall thought. *He's no longer interested in controlling the world. Right?* Marshall tried to get a read off his boss, but once again Sloane had gone all stoic on him.

"Good job, Marshall," Sloane said with a nod. "And Drew."

"Thank you, sir," Drew brownnosed excitedly. "Thank you."

"We'll report back when we find something," Marshall said as they exited the office.

"That went well," Drew said once they were out of earshot.

For once in his life Marshall had nothing to say.

CHAPTER 12

Sydney turned the black-and-white card over in her hand. She wasn't expecting to see anything other than the white star with the number thirteen in the center. She had examined it plenty of times since taking it from the dead hand of Stefani Martine. She still didn't know why she hadn't given it to Marshall earlier to assess at APO. Not that he would have had the time to look at it. The metal arm and Martine's files were going to be taking up a considerable amount of his attention for the fore-seeable future.

The card in her hand looked like nothing more than a simple business card. No different from the one she had gotten in Switzerland. But it didn't provide any *real* information. No real name. No address. No contact information of any kind.

Sydney couldn't help but recall the look on the man's face as he flew off in the helicopter. He was the one who had just committed a murder. Yet, by the way he stared, it seemed as though he were judging *her*. As though he had any idea who she was. Then again, she could just be paranoid. It wouldn't be the first time she thought the world was against her.

"We'll get 'em next time," Weiss said from the molded yellow plastic seat across from her. Sydney and Nadia were sitting side by side on the subway car, with Weiss across the aisle.

"Yeah," Sydney replied.

But Sydney wasn't exactly lamenting the fact that their mission had failed. She wasn't even wondering about the people behind Thirteen Stars anymore. She was more focused on that she had finally come to the conclusion that she was relieved Maximilian Sprague and Stefani Martine were dead.

Granted it was easier to accept the death of a creep like Sprague than a seemingly nice person like Martine. But at least someone had managed to cut off the source of horrific weaponry. Sydney silently wished that she could have been the one to put a stop to the team of arms dealers.

Wasn't that why I signed on for APO in the first place?

"Who do you think they are?" Nadia asked, looking at the card.

"Good question," Sydney replied simply. She wasn't worried about having the conversation in the subway car. The noise from the moving car would thwart anyone who could possibly be trying to over-hear them. Not to mention the fact that the car was moving through the L.A. underground. The only other people around were all the way on the other side of the car.

A grandmother and her young grandson sat beside each other expressing no interest in listen-ing to the conversation of a group of people dressed in fashionable business suits. The boy was loudly reading the comic off a Bazooka gum wrapper as if it were the funniest thing in the world. His grand-mother sat beside him nodding, with a forced smile indicating that it wasn't the first time she had heard the joke.

Otherwise the car was entirely empty. Nobody really used the L.A. subway system, especially in the middle of the day.

The sedan from the airport had dropped Sydney, Nadia, and Weiss off at their places before taking Vaughn home to freshen up quickly. It would have been less crowded if he had shared a car with Dixon, but Sydney suspected Vaughn knew she needed him around a bit longer. She realized that she had been in a funk lately, ever since Switzerland. Martine's death had just exacerbated Sydney's feelings of impotence over actually stopping so-called evildoers.

They were all set to reconvene at APO within the hour to go over the failed mission on board the *Triton*. Weiss had driven Sydney and her sister to the station nearest their homes. There they boarded a train together to ride in to work. Every now and then the team varied their approach to the office when they didn't go in during the normal morning rush. Little things like that helped keep the secret headquarters secret.

"Have you had the chance to think about tomorrow morning?" Nadia asked.

Sydney racked her brain, but she wasn't sure what Nadia was talking about. The confused look on Sydney's face must have given it away.

"The Omnifam meeting?" Nadia reminded her. "Coming along as emotional support?"

Sydney would have laughed at the idea of her providing emotional support for anyone at the moment, but she knew her sister wouldn't appreciate that. She had totally forgotten about the latest move in Sloane's ongoing PR campaign for redemption. In fact, she had hardly given it a moment's thought since Nadia had asked her the day before. But "sleeping" on the issue actually helped her see things more clearly. It really wasn't that big of a deal. There was no real reason for her to skip the event. It wasn't like Sloane would be less in her life if she missed it.

"Of course I'll go," Sydney said. "You did say something about breakfast afterward, right? I can always go for a free meal, you know."

Both women let out a small laugh at Sydney's joke. It really wasn't that funny, but the light-hearted comment helped relieve the pressure that neither of them had realized had entered the conversation.

A few minutes later the train stopped at their station. Sydney, Nadia, and Weiss departed, leaving the grandmother and child behind in the car waiting for the next passengers to board. The platform held only a few people waiting to be taken to their destinations, and they managed to board rather quickly.

The trio waited for the train to continue on its journey before they headed off the platform to the secret entrance to APO. When the platform was entirely empty, they could make their way to the entrance with only the security cameras watching. And since the cameras were the property of APO, they weren't a concern.

Weiss ran through the sequence of levers that opened the door to the APO offices. Being the gentleman, he ushered Nadia and Sydney into the hall before him.

"Here we are again, kiddies," Weiss said. "Another day, another—"

The door slammed shut behind them, faster than it ever had before. An alarm blared through the entry hall and red strobe lights started flashing.

"What's that?" Nadia asked as they looked around for a sign of attack or anything that would indicate what was going on.

"We'd better check it out," Weiss said.

The trio was about to move down the hall when the guard sitting at the security station came out from behind his desk and motioned for them to hold their positions. Sydney noticed that his gun was out of its holster. It wasn't aimed at them, but it was unnerving all the same.

"What's going on?" Sydney asked.

"You need to stay here, Ms. Bristow," the guard said. "I can't let you into the building until I receive the all clear."

"Look, Tim, it's us," Weiss said. "Remember? I just scored you prime seats to the Lakers game. This is some way to repay a guy."

But Tim didn't say anything. He just stood at the end of the hall, holding his gun at his side.

Sloane and Jack came around the corner and hurried into the entry hall. Marshall was trailing behind the men. Even though they were all moving at the same relative speed, Marshall's frantic mannerisms made it seem as though he were moving at a frenetic pace.

"Can someone please tell us what's going on?" Sydney asked as Marshall scanned Nadia with a small black device.

"Security picked up an unidentified transmission coming from one of you," Sloane said, eyeing Sydney and Weiss suspiciously. "Please hand over your cell phones and anything electronic on your persons."

"That's ridiculous," Weiss said as he gave his cell to Tim, who had holstered his gun but still stood at alert. "We're not transmitting anything."

"Nadia's clean," Marshall said.

"Try this," Sydney said as she handed over the business card she had taken from Martine's lifeless body. She didn't expect it to have any transmitter, but she had seen Marshall do amazing things with less to work with.

"Nope," Marshall said as he quickly scanned the card. "Nothing electronic in it at all."

"What kind of signal is it?" Nadia asked. "Are we bugged? Is someone listening in right now?"

"It's a simple monotonic signal," Marshall said as he slipped the business card into his jacket pocket and started scanning Sydney. "Like the repeated ping from a tracking device."

"Internal security can block any unauthorized outgoing transmissions," Jack said. "Either bugs or tracking signals. So we're safe for the moment."

"But if it's a tracking device, whoever's following it on the other end will just go to where they lost the signal," Sydney said. "We should—"

But the beeping from Marshall's scanner interrupted her. The device was currently aimed directly at the back of her neck.

"I don't believe it," Marshall said. "This can't be. . . . It's impossible."

"What is it, Marshall?" Sloane asked.

"It can't be," Marshall said.

"It can't be what?" Jack asked, with barely concealed annoyance.

"The Second Skin," Marshall said. "Somehow Syd's got the Second-Skin Tracker on her."

There was a pause as everyone took in the full ramifications of the statement.

"Well, get it off!" Weiss finally burst out.

"No," Sydney said. "If the signal stops here, it will lead them here. I have to lead whoever's tracking me away from APO."

"I thought that thing died at some point after Sprague's transmission," Nadia said.

"So did I," Marshall said. "Whoever took it off Sprague must have—I can't believe it—must have quickly examined my entirely unique and totally

one-of-a-kind technology and altered it so the sig-
nal would be sent to them instead of us. Wow.
That's so cool. I mean, bad. Really, really bad.
But . . . cool."

"It must be Thirteen Stars," Jack said.

"If it is, we've got some serious competition,"
Marshall admitted. "They've got one heck of a tech
guy—um—person, which makes me way more concerned about the seismic bomb casing being in
their possession."

"Seismic bomb?" Sydney asked.

"We'll fill you in later," Jack said. "First we
need to deal with the tracking device."

"How did it get on Sydney?" Nadia asked.

"When I was fighting that man on the ship,"
Sydney said, "he had me around the throat at one
point. He must have put it on then."

"Isn't this thing a bug, too?" Weiss asked. "Is
it recording everything we say right now to eventually send back to Thirteen Stars?"

"Marshall, when was the last scheduled transmission?" Jack asked.

Sydney tried to think back to everything she
had said since escaping the *Triton*. She was pretty
sure that they hadn't referred to APO by name

except in the last few minutes, but they had certainly used each other's names several times over the past few hours.

"Assuming they didn't have time to alter the burst transmission schedule," Marshall said, "and that would really take a work of pure and utter genius the likes of which do not exist on this planet—"

"Marshall," Sloane said with a calm anger.

"The last transmission would have occurred before it was placed on Syd," Marshall said. "Assuming they figured out how to intercept that too. It's on a different wavelength from the tracking signal. It's all very . . . technical. We're fine . . . except . . ."

"Except what?" Jack asked.

"The next transmission is scheduled for twenty minutes from now," Marshall said, checking his watch. "Actually eighteen minutes and thirty-five seconds . . . thirty-four . . . thirty-three . . ."

"So if I stay here," Sydney said, "they use the tracker to locate APO. But if I leave, they get a record of everything I've said since I left the ship."

"Can we keep the tracker active but jam the transmission?" Weiss asked.

Marshall seemed to consider the question.

"Marshall?" Sloane pressed.

"Yes . . . probably . . . maybe," Marshall said as he dashed down the hall. "I just need a few things from my lab!"

"Sydney, take the tracking device somewhere public and wait for someone from Thirteen Stars to contact you," Sloane said. "They are probably just as interested in us as we are in them. Weiss, you and Nadia go with Sydney. Keep her safe."

"What if they don't want to contact Sydney?" Nadia asked. "What if they want to hurt her?"

"They had plenty of opportunities before now," Sloane said. "They want something from her. They want to know who she's working for."

"Do you think they want to make a deal for this seismic bomb?" Sydney asked.

"I don't believe they're into making deals," Jack said. "From what I've learned, they have more of a single-minded approach to achieving their goals." Jack proceeded to fill them in on what his contact had told him about the vigilante organization. It took Sydney a moment to process that their new enemy wasn't necessarily the collection of bad guys she thought they were.

As Jack wrapped up his brief, Marshall came running back down the hall. His arms were loaded with tools and technology. He had thrown a backpack on too, but hadn't even taken the time to fill it before coming back to them. "Okay, I think I have everything. Well, not *everything* everything but everything I'm going to need to block the transmission. I think."

"You'd better get moving," Jack said. "Before someone comes looking for you."

"I can continue to block the tracking signal with this"—Marshall held up a small silver and black box—"until Syd gets out of the subway. That way whoever's on the other end thinks it was just the underground interference that blocked the signal."

"Give me the business card," Jack said to Marshall, who had pocketed the card after Sydney gave it to him.

"Um . . . a little help?" Marshall asked, nodding down to his jacket pocket. His arms were too full for him to get anything out.

Since Weiss was the closest, he reached into Marshall's left jacket pocket, pulled out the card, and handed it to Jack.

"Be careful," Sloane said. "We don't know who we're dealing with."

"Let's go," Sydney said, and they left the office once the guard gave them the all clear from his desk overlooking the security cameras.

Sydney waited on the platform for the next train to come by. Glancing left, she saw Nadia and Weiss stationed by the escalators in case her mysterious tracker came in looking for her. Marshall was sitting at a bench working on his frequency jammer. It was noticeably out of place for him to be working on it in a train station, but they didn't have time to worry about appearances. They were fifteen minutes away from blowing their covers and effectively destroying APO.

Sydney reached into her blazer pocket and pulled out the earbud and communications device she had used on the *Triton*. She slipped it into her ear and performed a quick verbal cue to confirm that Weiss, Nadia, and Marshall had all done the same.

She doubted that whoever was tracking her would come search for her in the subway. She had only been there for a few minutes. No one had made contact with her when she had stopped at home, and she had been there for about a half hour. Of course, that could just mean Thirteen Stars now had her home address and could use that information later. She assumed that she would have to remain stationary for at least an hour before whoever was tracking her made contact.

The Metro Red Line car pulled up to the platform. Sydney waited as the passengers emptied out of the car. This one was a little more crowded than the one she had taken in to work.

Weiss and Nadia came up behind Sydney and followed her into the subway car. Marshall had been so focused on his task that he almost missed the car entirely. It took a quiet prompt from Weiss to rouse Marshall from his work so he could board the train.

Sydney cased the car as she entered. It would have been nearly impossible for anyone tracking her to be on that train or in that specific car, but she never let her defenses down for a moment. The car held a young couple, a trio of elderly women, and several apparent day laborers who looked like they had just gotten off a morning shift.

None of the group looked to be a particular threat. Then again, Sydney had dressed up as everything from a geisha to an elderly Mexican woman before. In her line of work, a threat could come from the most unlikely of sources. As such, she remained prepared in case an attack did come.

The ride was a short one. The train only made a few stops to let several people on and off as it rolled toward Union Station. Sydney wasn't going that far, though. She had already come up with a good public place to go in the middle of the day.

Sydney exited the train at the Pershing Square Station. She was about to take the stairs up to street level, when Marshall chimed in over the communicator.

"Hold on, Syd," Marshall said. She could hear him tinkering with the technology as he spoke to her. "The recorded transmission is about to go out to whoever's listening. I think I can intercept it, but you should stay underground until we're clear."

"Are you still blocking the tracking device?" Sydney asked.

"Yes . . . I think," Marshall said.

"As soon as we're clear you need to let them see that the tracking device is active again," Sydney said. "Or they're going to start looking in the last place it was transmitting from and they could find headquarters."

"I'm on it," Marshall said as a hum came over the communications system. Apparently the interference on the Second Skin was also going to mess with their ability to communicate with one another. "Here we go."

Sydney went over to a newsstand so she wasn't too exposed while standing around the subway station. The hum in her ear grew louder, to the point where she began to worry that the guy running the newsstand could hear it. He didn't say anything, but he spent his days working in a subway station, so she figured he witnessed stranger things on a daily basis.

As the hum continued to increase in volume, Sydney wished she could take the communications device out of her ear but knew it was best to stay in contact. Weiss had already gone ahead to secure the exit, and Nadia was keeping an eye on incoming trains. If anything unexpected occurred, they would need to know immediately.

If they can get a message through the interference, she thought.

After a minute the hum began to dissipate. It

took another minute and a half for it to totally disappear.

"I got it," Marshall said, sounding more surprised than Sydney liked to hear. "I managed to intercept the recording and download it into the jammer. We're in the clear."

"Okay then," Sydney said. "Put me back on their radar."

"Tracker's hot," Marshall said over the comm.

Sydney took the stairs and headed for the exit with Marshall and Nadia following. All three of them passed Weiss as they stepped out into the downtown L.A. sunshine.

Pershing Square was busy for the midwinter afternoon but not quite busy enough that Sydney felt comfortable waiting there for Thirteen Stars to contact her. She had something else in mind.

Though the sun was shining, it was still a bit chilly. That meant the locals weren't heading outside en masse to enjoy the day. Anywhere else in the country, people would be dying for weather like this in January. But anytime L.A. residents were forced to throw on a light jacket, it was tantamount to asking them to go out in a blizzard. Besides, even on the most beautiful day in existence, downtown Los Angeles wasn't exactly a hotbed of activity.

Sydney needed people . . . and additional security wouldn't hurt either. There were several options for that in the area, like the L.A. County Courthouse. But Sydney didn't want to make things too difficult for her trackers. She wanted Thirteen Stars to make contact, not to scare them away by going someplace that was too secure.

Heading a block up Sixth Street to South Grand Avenue, she turned right. The streets were empty enough that she knew Weiss, Nadia, and Marshall could keep her easily in sight. She didn't even bother to glance back to make sure they were following. They would keep her safe.

It was only a couple blocks before she saw the oddly shaped building she was heading toward. This wasn't the first time she had seen it, but it still looked weird to her. It looked as if the architect had lost all sense of perspective when designing it.

The Museum of Contemporary Art, better known as MOCA, had a considerable number of people milling about outside for midday in the middle of the week. This was a good sign that inside would be just as populated. It never failed to surprise Sydney the number of people around Los Angeles who did not seem to have jobs during the day.

"Anyone feel like an afternoon of fine art?" Sydney asked as she made her way to the entrance.

"*Contemporary* art," Weiss corrected over the comm. "We're talking blotches of color on canvases or a statue that's just a phone booth. There's nothing *fine* about it."

Art criticism aside, it was the perfect place to go to be seen.

"I'm going to patch into base ops," Marshall said, "see if someone can get us linked into the surveillance system."

Sydney did not reply. She was buying her ticket into the museum and assumed that it would look odd if she started talking to herself. Then she noticed a few scraggy-haired artist-types over at the side of the building. They were collected in a bunch but none of them seemed to be with the others. The one thing they all had in common—aside from their crazy artiste appearances—was that they all seemed to be talking to themselves.

A visit to MOCA was always different from a

visit to one of the museums in the area that housed more traditional artwork. Weiss was right about the broader definition of "art" that MOCA subscribed to, but Sydney wasn't going to let him know that. She had been surprisingly moved by some of the stranger compositions that she had seen over the years at MOCA. But she wasn't going to let Weiss know that, either.

A group of high school students in line behind Sydney were openly staring at the odd collection of mumbling artist-types. The teens seemed too confused by the men to say anything mean. Sydney briefly wondered if they were an exhibit. She figured the kids were wondering that too.

Though she hadn't commented on Marshall connecting with APO, the next voice she heard in her ear was very reassuring.

"We're patched in," her father said as Marshall connected with APO. "And Vaughn is on his way to the location as well."

Sydney was especially glad to hear that last part. Not that she didn't have enough backup for what she expected would be a simple meet, but anyone who could secretly board a cruise ship, commit a very public murder, and be extracted by a helicopter was definitely someone she wanted to be fully prepared for.

"The surveillance cameras are on a closed system," Sloane added. "We won't be able to access them remotely. But I expect we can obtain a copy of the video afterward."

Sydney waited and followed the school group into the building and down the entrance hall. Once she had determined where they were going, she turned into one of the exhibit rooms to the side. She knew that there would be kids in the building but preferred to avoid putting them in the line of potential fire. The room she chose had rows of jagged black-and-white sculptures and stark paintings on the wall. Even though tour groups would continue in and out of the room as she waited, she couldn't imagine any of the children wanting to lag behind. There were far more colorful kid-friendly pieces throughout the museum to capture their attention.

"What now?" Marshall asked softly as he came into the room and positioned himself beneath a silver metal mobile. Nadia had gone for the other exit from the room, while Weiss stayed outside the entrance she had come in.

"Now? We wait," Sydney said as she took a seat on the bench in front of a painting that was simply rows of black and gray stripes in descending shades, save a small red dot in the lower right-hand corner. She passed the time by trying to figure out what the artist had been thinking when he created the piece. Nothing immediately sprang to mind that resembled what Sydney would have considered any kind of serious thought.

At least it helped occupy her mind while she waited to meet with a man who had been strangling her only fourteen hours earlier.

CHAPTER 13

MUSEUM OF CONTEMPORARY ART
LOS ANGELES

Sydney waited in the MOCA exhibit hall for some-one from Thirteen Stars to make contact. The black-and-white art all around her was a constant reminder of the Thirteen Stars business cards she kept finding around the world. She had been to Switzerland, Peru, and on a cruise ship in the last couple days and was really beginning to feel like she needed a vacation.

At roughly a half hour into the wait, Vaughn entered the hall and took a seat on the bench across the room behind Sydney. He didn't bother to approach her in case she was being watched, but he wasn't hiding either.

It was likely that the man Sydney fought on the *Triton* would be the one making contact. Since the guy knew what Vaughn looked like, the fact that Vaughn was sitting in plain sight made it clear that he wasn't about to let anything happen to Sydney. Being seated across from her instead of beside her also sent the message that he was watching but he wasn't going to get in the way.

Another half hour passed before the man Sydney had fought on the *Triton* appeared in the room. Sydney recognized him immediately. He was carrying a messenger bag, which was a bit of a concern. No telling what could be inside. Even though he did have to go through a security check to get into the museum, he could have had any number of items in the bag that would seem harmless but could prove deadly. She had used enough of Marshall's toys over the past decade to know that particular danger.

The man took a few steps into the exhibit hall and paused as if daring the security cameras to pick him up. In fact, he appeared to be seeking out each of the video cameras to make sure they got a good shot.

Sydney sat up straighter as she waited for him to make his approach. She glanced back to Vaughn and noticed his fist sliding in the direction of his holstered gun. It was clear he wanted payback for the sneak attack on the ship. But Sydney knew he wouldn't do anything to jeopardize the fact-finding mission, and certainly nothing that would put the innocents in the room at risk.

The mystery man surveyed the room, his eyes stopping briefly on Vaughn before continuing. It was unlikely that he'd made Nadia or Marshall, or Weiss out in the hallway, but she assumed the man figured she and Vaughn were not alone. Sydney slid to the side of the bench, allowing room for the man. After a moment he walked over to her and took the space offered.

"Ms. Bristow," he said warmly as he sat. "Good to see you again."

Sydney was well practiced at keeping her facial features locked to hide her emotions. But she knew her eyes gave away the surprise at being so easily identified.

"That your buddy from the ship over there?" the man asked nonchalantly. "His hair's lighter. Figure there's more of you guys hanging around too, huh?"

"We've got the place covered," Sydney said. "Mr. . . ?"

"You can figure that out later from the security cameras," the man said lightly. "Can't make things too easy on you. By the way, I've got a friend or two here myself." He nodded in the direction of the door and a blond woman who looked like the one Marshall and Dixon had described having a run-in with.

"Then we should get down to business," Sydney said. "I think we each have something the other wants."

"You mean that metal thingy your friends stole from the ship?" the man said. "You can keep it."

This meet was getting stranger by the second. Sydney had expected him to come to her with some kind of offer. Marshall had filled her in a bit on the technology while they waited. They were dealing with powerful stuff. She wondered if the man was playing a game with her. "But why did you go to the trouble—"

"We've got the rest of the device," the man said. "It's okay if it's missing a piece. We don't plan to use it."

"The people I work for *are* interested in the

device," Sydney said, figuring someone needed to offer a deal to keep the conversation going. She had to find an opening to make a play for the bomb casing. If it really was as powerful as Marshall had said it was, APO needed to be in control of the device.

Correction: The CIA needed to have control of it, she thought.

"Now, there's an interesting question," the man said. "Who exactly *are* your people? I know you and the CIA recently . . . severed ties. But I'm wondering who snapped you up so fast."

"You seem to know a lot about me," Sydney said.

"Not as much as I'd like," the man said.

"Such as?"

"Such as how did you get yourself mixed up with people like Maximilian Sprague and Stefani Martine?" he asked. "Those aren't exactly the kinds of people you should be doing business with."

"They had what I was looking for," Sydney replied. "They were willing to make a deal. In case you hadn't noticed, I'm in the business to make deals."

"Yeah, you'd better not wait up on those Scorpion Pistols, by the way," the man said. "We've taken care of that shipment. Took care of Sprague, too."

"So I'd heard," Sydney said. "Doesn't really matter. I was done with him, anyway. Just out of curiosity, what did he do to you? Why did you kill him?"

"He didn't do anything to me," the man said, "except make the world I live in a more dangerous place."

"Some would say the world was already dangerous," Sydney said, playing into the character the mystery man had created for her. "Some would also say that he was simply providing a means to make it safer for those open to doing business with him."

"Some?" he asked. "Meaning you?"

"Me," she replied. "Or . . ."

"The people you work for," he concluded.

She flashed him a smile.

"You might want to check this out," the man said as he reached into his messenger bag and pulled out a manila envelope. "It's some interesting reading on your old friend Maximilian Sprague."

"I never said that we were friends," Sydney

insisted, with more emotion than she had intended. She held on to the envelope but didn't bother to look inside. She didn't want him to think that she was too interested in Maximilian Sprague. And honestly, she wasn't really. The only thing she did want to know is why the man had been motivated to kill Sprague.

"Look, Ms. Bristow," the man said. "Sydney . . ."

That caught her off guard. There was something almost fatherly in the way he spoke her name. Not quite as intimate as when Sloane spoke it, but there was definitely a familiar air to the way he addressed her. Her mind went into overdrive thinking of the many contacts she'd had in the past, but his face certainly didn't ring any bells.

"You seem to have fallen in with a bad element," he continued. "I get that. The CIA has been known to frustrate even its most valued officers. I just never thought someone with your record would turn so quickly."

"Turn?" Sydney asked. She picked up on the slight catch in his voice when he spoke about the CIA. It was an obvious clue that she debated whether or not to pursue at the moment.

"I guess it's not really a big surprise," the man

said. "I mean, you did work for SD-6 for a long time. Maybe some of that rubbed off."

"I don't know how—"

"Still," the man continued, "didn't think you'd start dabbling in freelance terrorism. Especially so soon after you left the Agency."

Sydney shouldn't have been stunned that he had leapt to that conclusion. Based on the facts he had available to him, it was a logical conclusion. That *was* the part she was playing, the alias she had taken. Normal civilians didn't go around every day making deals for shipments of weapons. Still, she was tempted to correct the man's misinterpretation of her motives. But it wasn't as if she could just explain that she was working for a black ops government agency.

She also didn't know why his opinion of her even mattered.

"Or maybe you're not freelance," the man said. "Maybe you're working for your old boss."

"My—"

"Sloane," he said. "Oh, you don't think I bought that act of him turning all good and starting up some relief organization? What kind of a fool do you think I am? Arvin Sloane is up to something.

And if you're working for him, I have to wonder what it is that got you back into his fold. Did he make you an offer you couldn't resist?"

"You're jumping to a lot of conclusions," Sydney said. His intensity both scared her and piqued her interest. There was a clue in the way he spoke about Sloane. The video cameras around the room would help provide some answers later.

"I'm working with the facts as I see them," the man replied.

"Isn't it possible that Maximilian Sprague was just a distant relative I was looking up?" Sydney teased. "Maybe Stefani Martine was a long-lost cousin?"

The man laughed out loud. It echoed through the quiet room, causing several art patrons to turn and glare in his direction.

"I like you," he said, ignoring the people glaring at him. "Which is one of the reasons I'm not going to kill you."

"That's nice to know," Sydney said dryly. "Of course, I think that has more to do with the number of guns discreetly pointed in your direction at the moment than any feelings you may have for me. But it's nice to know I'm safe."

"Today," he quickly added. "I'm not going to kill you *today*. But if you get in my way again, that might change."

"Maybe if you gave me an idea of your agenda, I'd know how to avoid you," Sydney said. "Make sure we don't show up at the same events wearing the same outfits. That sort of thing."

"I noticed you took my card from Martine back on the ship," the man said.

"Yes."

"Do your research," the man said. "If you're as good as I hear you are, why don't you come lookin' for me? Maybe you'll be interested in joining up. Become our thirteenth member. I kind of like the symmetry in that."

"Certainly something to think about," Sydney said. She knew he wouldn't answer if she asked him again about his organization. She debated referring to it by name, but she didn't want to give him too much of the upper hand. It was better if he thought she was clueless as to the motivations behind Thirteen Stars. "Are you sure you don't want to hear my offer for the seismic—"

"Nope," the man said as he stood. "We're fine. Just wanted to stop by to warn you off."

"Well, thanks," Sydney said as she rose.

"I don't suppose you'd like to give me back that impressive piece of technology stuck on your neck at the moment," the man said. "My tech guy nearly passed out with excitement when he examined it."

"No, I think I'll keep it," Sydney replied, and caught the smug look on Marshall's face across the room. "*My* tech guy doesn't like me sharing his toys."

Like she was just going to hand over the Second Skin simply because the guy had asked.

"I understand," the man said. "Oh, and one other thing." As he spoke, the warm smile faded and his face set in a grim look. "If you *are* working for Arvin Sloane again, I'd suggest finding another employer. It's not a good career move."

"Believe me when I say you don't need to tell me that."

Sydney watched as the man walked out of the room.

"That's it?" Vaughn asked over the comm. "Should we take him?"

"Negative," Marshall said. "That *is* his friend from the ship waiting out in the hall. Wow. Even from this far away, I can see the lump she got when

I clocked her." There was a definite note of pride in his voice.

"We've got an agent tracking him out of the museum," Sloane said over the comm from APO headquarters. "Merlin, obtain the museum security video. We've sent a car to pick you up. Everyone else, come back to base."

As soon as they knew the room was clear, Vaughn rushed to Sydney's side. She wanted badly to hug him, but she was trying to maintain some professional decorum.

"You okay?" he asked.

"I didn't expect him to know so much about me," Sydney replied.

"We'll get him on video," Vaughn reassured her. "Then we'll know all about *him*."

Weiss also noticed that Sydney seemed a little shaken. Without mentioning that, he offered that he and Nadia could help Marshall speak with security so Sydney and Vaughn could ride back together. It was an especially good idea, since Marshall wasn't always the best when dealing with authority figures. But Sydney also appreciated that Weiss could be counted on to know when she needed some alone time.

Before they left, Sydney handed the Second Skin to Marshall, who finally disabled it. Considering their own technology had almost been used against them, maybe it was a little too good.

"Sloane has someone watching your house," Vaughn said as they left the museum. "But he and your father doubt that anyone will try to make contact with you there."

Sydney knew he was trying to reassure her, but she suspected that since she'd stopped at her place, Thirteen Stars had it targeted in case they changed their minds about keeping her alive. "Just the same, would you mind if I stayed at your place tonight?"

"Not at all," Vaughn said with a grin.

"Nadia should stay somewhere too," Sydney said. "For tonight at least."

"Well, she could bunk with Weiss," Vaughn said, grinning more broadly.

Sydney had noticed a definite attraction between the pair, but it was still a little early in the relationship to suggest anything like that. As far as Sydney knew, they hadn't even been on a date yet. "Now, Vaughn, what kind of a girl do you take my sister for?"

They finally reached Vaughn's SUV, which was parked in a public structure a block away. It seemed as though they were totally alone on that level of the lot. After Vaughn opened her door for her, he pulled her into an embrace. It surprised Sydney to realize how much she needed it at the moment.

"Are you really okay?" he asked as they broke apart and got into the SUV. "I didn't realize that meet was so intense for you."

"It wasn't," Sydney said. "It's just . . . It's not every day I'm mistaken for a terrorist."

"Well, this mystery guy just doesn't know you," Vaughn said as he started the SUV and pulled out of the spot.

"Maybe he knows me too well," Sydney said. "How do we really know we're doing any good? We make deals with the bad guys. We ignore the law."

"We go in where the CIA can't," Vaughn said. "That doesn't make us evil. Everything we do is under the approval of Director Chase."

"International law exists for a reason," Sydney said. "Who are we to just bypass it whenever we please? Maximilian Sprague and Stefani Martine are dead. Ultimately you can make the argument that that's a good thing. But somehow it's bad for us. It gets in the way of our plan. Does that even make sense?"

"Look, Syd, we don't deal in absolutes," Vaughn reminded her. "This is not a simple matter of the bad guys wear black hats and the good guys wear white."

"I'm just tired of living in different shades of gray," Sydney said as she opened the envelope the man had given her. She went silent as she looked over the contents.

"What is it?" Vaughn asked as he drove through downtown L.A.

"A darker shade of gray," Sydney replied.

The front page of the local Bern newspaper had a huge banner headline. Translated into English it would read, DEADLIEST DAY IN HISTORY. Ignoring what she hoped was hyperbole, the first thing Sydney noticed were the photos. There were two, side-by-side. On the left was of a pair of body bags in the Bear Pits, one of Bern's most famous attractions.

Sydney had no clue what that picture was in reference to. The other photo was more familiar. It was another pair of body bags lying by one of the city's other famous attractions, the Ogre Fountain.

She knew exactly who was in those bags.

Sydney had enough of a handle on the language to get the gist of the article. Bern wasn't a particularly violent town. So imagine the shock when four people were found murdered within one hour. All four had been shot, and the police could tell that their deaths were somehow linked.

The article began with a touching story about a young couple that had been visiting the town's famed Bear Pits. Even though the bears had been hibernating, the man brought his girlfriend there to re-create the first date they'd had together a year-and-a-half earlier. According to his family he had intended to propose to her. Police confirmed this when they found the ring still in his pocket. He had never had the chance to give it to her. Apparently they had stumbled across something they shouldn't have seen.

Instead of starting a life together, the young couple had been murdered by someone who had gotten away. The time of their death was roughly the time that Sydney had been scheduled to meet with Maximilian Sprague. The meaning was clear. They had been murdered by Sprague.

It was rumored that during the off-season the

Bear Pits made for a convenient place for the local criminal element to meet. The paper was referring to small-time crooks and drug dealers, but Sydney knew that on that day a larger-scale criminal had been there. The writer of the article assumed that the couple had stumbled across a drug deal in progress. Sydney figured that was half-right. The couple had certainly stumbled across some kind of meeting.

The article went on to talk about the two unidentified men found where Sydney had left them. Police had linked the two crimes because bullets in the guns found on the two men matched the ones used to kill the young couple.

Sydney remembered back to Sprague showing up ten minutes late to their meet. His jovial attitude had bothered her at the time. Now it sickened her. He had come straight from a murder and then acted flirtatiously with her while making their deal; it was disgusting. But Sydney wasn't just thinking ill of the dead, she was equally sick with herself.

Instead of punishing the man, who had countless acts of additional violence in his files, Sydney had made a deal with him. She had deposited a significant amount of money into his account.

Money that he would have used to build more weapons that would kill more innocent people. Money that was probably still being used by the surviving members of his organization.

Sydney hadn't stopped him. She hadn't even tried. The only reason he wasn't on the streets at the moment was because Thirteen Stars had done what she hadn't been allowed to do.

Attached to the article was another card with the white star and the number thirteen in the center. Sydney turned the card over. A note was scribbled on the back, obviously intended for her. It read: "Let me know if you get tired of doing business with people like this."

CHAPTER 14

Within the hour, the team reconvened in the APO conference room. Dixon was brought up to speed on what he had missed during his short jaunt home. For reasons Sydney still didn't understand, Dixon apologized for not getting back earlier, as if he should have known what was going on. Besides, he had a perfect reason to delay his return to work, as far as Sydney was concerned.

Dixon had swung by his kids' school to visit them during lunch. It was a little out of the ordinary to do such a thing, but he couldn't wait to see them. It was just another thing that made Sydney both love her friend and worry for him, considering that he was going through the same moral dilemma as she was, working for Sloane again.

"You knew about the people in Bern. The couple Sprague had killed," Sydney accused Sloane right out of the gate. She wasn't angry just for herself but for Dixon and the rest of the team as well. It wasn't the best way to start a meeting, but Sydney had a bad history with surprises.

Sloane nodded his head in confirmation.

"Is there a reason you didn't tell us about it?" Sydney asked.

"We have been rather busy since I heard the news," Sloane said. "Considering it didn't have any impact on the mission, there seemed no point in mentioning it."

An emergency phone call from Director Chase interrupted before Sydney could respond to their very different interpretations of the importance of full disclosure. Sloane's assistant had the director patched into the conference room. Apparently it was something that could affect everyone in the room.

"We've had a security breach," Chase said as

soon as she was on speaker. "Someone hacked into the CIA mainframe about an hour ago."

Sydney checked her watch out of habit. She didn't need to see the current time to make the connection. The hack had happened while she was meeting with the mystery man. It wasn't a coincidence.

"What did they get?" Sloane asked.

"Not much," Chase replied. "Our techs managed to close the backdoor they used to get in as soon as the system's alarm went off. But they weren't just out for a joyride on the government's information highway. They were looking for a specific file."

"Let me guess," Sydney said. "Mine."

"No, actually," Chase replied. "Sloane's."

Sydney was just as surprised as everyone else in the room over that revelation.

"Does that mean . . . ," Marshall started to say. "I'm sorry, Director Chase, it's me, Marshall, speaking . . . Does that mean someone knows about APO?"

"No," Chase replied. "Any information about APO is kept on a separate server not networked to the system in any way. It would be impossible to access it from the outside. And only a handful of people have clearance to even know about it on the inside."

"Then what did they get?" Dixon asked.

"Everything related to Sloane's . . . previous line of work," Chase replied.

"I suspect that you are not referring to my time with Omnifam," Sloane said, attempting to sound lighthearted but not quite making it.

"Basically it was your life before the creation of APO," Chase said. "Prior CIA involvement . . . SD-6 . . . personal history. We're trying to back-trace the hack. Hopefully it will lead us to who-ever is interested in you."

Sydney doubted they were going to find any-thing. If Thirteen Stars' tech guy could adapt Marshall's Second Skin technology in a matter of hours, he could probably manage a simple hack without leaving any evidence behind.

"We think we might already know who is involved," Sloane replied. "We'll contact you when we have more information."

Sydney didn't like that Sloane seemed to be cutting off Director Chase. She also didn't under-stand why he wasn't going to mention what they had learned about Thirteen Stars. She wanted to speak up herself but knew that it would not go over well at all if she did.

Sloane had a way of making things personal, and their current mission seemed to be getting more and more intimate as they progressed. She could tell by the silence on the other end of the line that Chase was debating with herself about how much string to give Sloane before she pulled him back.

"See that you do," she finally said, and as she severed the connection. Apparently, she had decided to give him some more leeway.

"This new information is not our priority," Sloane said as he stood. "The larger issue is that, whether they know it or not, someone is interfering with our work. That, and the fact that they have the larger component of an impressive piece of weapons technology, should be our focus."

Sydney couldn't help but think that once they took care of this mysterious Thirteen Stars organization, it would also take care of the stolen information from Sloane's files. She chose not to bother commenting. It would have been a waste of time, anyway.

Prior to the call from Director Chase, Marshall

had updated everyone on the full nature of the seismic bomb. Sydney wouldn't have used the word "impressive" to describe the horrific device, but it was quite a technological accomplishment.

She figured the dangerous bomb was a bit more of a concern than that Thirteen Stars was interfering with APO's missions. Although the man had said that he had no interest in using the seismic bomb, Sydney doubted he could be trusted, especially if he ever managed to gain possession of the core.

"What about the tail we had on the man from the museum?" Vaughn asked. "Have we found their headquarters?"

"Unfortunately we lost him around Chinatown," Sloane said. "We suspect he was on to our agents from the start and was just leading them around to waste time until he saw an opportunity to get away. The route he took was circuitous, to say the least. We have no idea where he was actually headed."

"So where does that leave us?" Dixon asked.

"Jack." Sloane nodded to Sydney's father as he took his seat.

Jack Bristow punched a button on the keypad in front of him, and an image from the MOCA security cameras was thrown onto the screen. It was a picture of the man Sydney had met with. The image was particularly clear, as he was looking directly into the camera.

"Harrison Cabot," Jack said as he hit another button that brought up a posed picture of the man. It looked like an image from a driver's license or a photo ID. "Former CIA operative."

"So that's how he knew Syd," Marshall said. "Did you guys ever work together? I don't recognize him."

"Actually," Jack said, looking directly at his daughter, "he knew Sydney through me."

Sydney remained silent. This wasn't the first time her father had dropped a bombshell in a meeting. At least this one seemed minor compared to some of the things she had learned in the past. Sometimes coincidences popped up in the espionage game. A simple look around the room showed just what a small world it was in their line of work.

"I worked with Harrison on occasion while I was stationed in Washington," Jack said. "Right before we moved to L.A. Cabot was new to the CIA. Green, but it was clear he was going to go far. He had a knack for counterstrategizing. Cabot could look over a situation and come up with a mission plan in seconds. He was always thinking. Always theorizing."

"Sounds like your kind of guy," Weiss said to Jack.

"If you knew him," Marshall connected the dots, "then you must have known him too, Mr. Sloane."

"That is correct," Sloane said. "He reported directly to me, actually. We worked very closely for a time while I was in the CIA."

Sydney couldn't hold her tongue. "So now this is a personal thing?" It made sense, considering the anger she had sensed in Cabot's voice when he spoke about Sloane.

"It is possible," Sloane said calmly, "that by stumbling across your involvement in this mission Cabot has had some old issues resurface."

"Such as?" Sydney asked.

She couldn't help but notice that Sloane glanced in Nadia's direction. This likely meant that he was about to admit to something that no one in the room—save, possibly, his daughter—was going to find surprising in the least.

"One of my first acts as head of SD-6," Sloane said, "was to order the execution of Cabot's partner, Kyle Swenson."

Sydney could see Nadia was trying hard not to react. Though her sister had seen Sloane's files, it was still hard to hear the truth from his mouth. Sydney found it difficult herself from time to time to listen to yet another admission of guilt. And she had known about Sloane's dark side for years.

"It was soon after the Alliance was formed," Sloane explained. "Swenson was—"

"Save the backstory," Jack said. He was clearly taking the temperature of the room and realized what Sydney knew. No one cared to have Sloane explain away another of his past acts. "The important part here is that Cabot thinks Sydney is working for Sloane again."

"Not that far from the truth," Weiss piped in.

Sydney wanted to smack her friend, but she knew he was just saying it blithely. It wasn't his fault that she was having such a problem dealing with the decision she had already made.

"Be that as it may," Jack added, "this could prove a threat to the continued existence of APO. If he keeps digging and finds the link between the two of them, he could trace it back to this organization."

"A group like Thirteen Stars could use the existence of APO to embarrass the government," Dixon added.

"What is Cabot up to now?" Vaughn asked. "Has he gone rogue too . . . I mean, like he thinks Sydney has?"

"In a way," Jack said, hitting another button on the keyboard. The symbol of the star with the number thirteen replaced Cabot's face on the screens. "As I learned in Washington, the files simply listing Thirteen Stars as a terrorist organization did not tell the whole story. They are a well organized vigilante group of about a dozen members set to keep the government on what they believe to be the 'straight and narrow.'"

Sydney thought back to Cabot's offer and how she would be the thirteenth member of the team. Suddenly his offer wasn't as offensive as it had been during their meet. He thought he was suggesting a more noble line of work for her. In a way, he was trying to save her from what she was afraid of becoming.

"It appears now that Cabot formed the organization," Jack said.

"So he just got tired of working for the government and decided to go into business on his own?" Vaughn asked.

"What happened?" Nadia asked. "What made him go rogue?"

"I did," Sloane said, to the surprise of no one.

"Shortly after his partner . . . died," Jack continued, "Cabot left the CIA. He had been working day and night to stop the newly formed SD-6 and Alliance. But while his motives were noble, his methods were barely making a dent. Even worse, his investigation into Sloane was jeopardizing *my* cover in SD-6. The CIA called him off the case."

"And he didn't like that," Weiss concluded.

"He fought it at first," Jack continued. "But eventually gave up. He went off the grid for several years. It was rumored that he was working as a bounty hunter. He would take on high-profile targets that met some very specific criteria. His targets were criminals that the government was not actively investigating. People he felt needed to be brought to justice.

"He would fund his work through criminals involved in turf wars," Jack went on. "This is where he excelled at intricate strategies. He would get someone to hire him to kill an enemy. Once his employer's enemy was dead, Cabot would collect his money. Then he would find another enemy of that same employer. He would go to that enemy and offer to kill his former employer for a fee. He continued down the line as he took out all his old bosses and targeted new ones while they paid him to do what he would have done for free."

"The enemy of my enemy is my assassin," Weiss added.

"Genius," Marshall said. "In a sick and twisted sort of way."

"A few years ago the FBI received reports that Cabot was forming a team," Jack said. "A group that was created to deal with people Cabot didn't feel the government was properly addressing."

"This team wouldn't have been formed around the time that, say, Omnifam was created?" Vaughn asked.

This time Sydney noticed that everyone was looking at Sloane.

"You can imagine how it might have upset Cabot to learn that I had changed my ways—" Sloan started to say.

Sydney cut him off. "Even more so because as

far as the public was concerned, you were some great humanitarian, while Cabot knew about all the crimes you had gotten away with."

"I made my penance," Sloane said. "The government granted my forgiveness."

"Cabot hasn't," Sydney said. She would have brought up the fact that Sloane hadn't *made* his penance so much as bought it, but that was a conversation for another time.

"Which brings us to our current dilemma," Jack said. "Thirteen Stars has been functioning on a small scale over the years. Cabot was wise to start his people off on small jobs. Get them used to the idea of vigilantism. The CIA didn't even know for sure they existed. The FBI looked at them only as a nuisance. Not a serious threat. But now they're interfering with the government's plans."

"Specifically, *our* plans," Sloane said to underscore that they were a government agency and he was in charge.

"But it's not like they really did anything wrong," Nadia said. "Sprague and Martine were—"

"The government's responsibility," Jack cut her off. "We can't afford to have an organization based in America enforcing policy wherever it pleases."

"Nope," Sydney said, eyeing Sloane again. "Can't have that."

"Sydney, please," her father said, causing Sydney to rein it in. "As noble as some may feel the efforts of Thirteen Stars to be, they are a vigilante group. The *have* committed murders. And they must be dealt with."

"But the FBI hasn't dealt with them for years," Sydney reminded her father.

"Yes, but Thirteen Stars has apparently stepped up their mission," Jack said. "These cards they're leaving around. They want to go public."

"They've already gone public if you consider the way Stefani Martine was killed," Vaughn added.

"But if you just consider that a warm-up," Jack said, "think about what could happen when they do it for real. By then we will have only ourselves to blame for not stopping them."

"Especially since they have part of Martine's weapon," Marshall chimed in. "The seismic bomb would be a pretty big way to make a statement."

"They can't use it without the other component," Sydney said, recalling what Cabot had told her at the museum. "And they don't intend to use it either, if Cabot can be believed."

"Which is open to interpretation," Sloane added. "We don't know their real intentions. And even if they are pure now, who is to say that they might not change their minds and make a play for the missing component at some point in the future? I can't think of a better way to take out a foreign enemy government."

"So why don't we destroy the core?" Nadia asked. "According to Marshall, Martine's files don't have anything on the core. Once it's gone, the seismic bomb is useless."

"If Martine could build it, someone else will most certainly find a way to recreate it," Sloane said. "It would be better for the government to have control of the device so we can determine how to stop another one."

Sydney wasn't buying the logic. Martine was a genius, which is why APO was originally going to approach her to work for the CIA. Even Marshall was in awe of the woman's abilities. The likelihood of another one of these seismic bombs being built did not outweigh the risk of someone stealing the core from the CIA. When Sydney thought of the number of times Rambaldi artifacts had been stolen back and forth over the years—and those were highly secured items—she found Sloane's logic to be incredibly flawed.

"Once we get the outer casing, what are we going to do with the Thirteen Stars operatives?" Sydney asked. "Do we take them in? Other than Cabot's admission of his involvement in the deaths of Sprague and Martine, do we have any evidence on the rest of his team? What are the charges? Conspiracy?"

"To commit murder," Sloane reminded her. "Yes, the files are incomplete. It is likely the FBI has more information on Thirteen Stars than we've had access to. But it does appear that they have been responsible for a number of murders over the years."

"Assassinations," Sydney corrected. "Of people the government would have gotten around to eventually. Some would say that Thirteen Stars was just saving us the work."

Sydney knew that people couldn't just go around killing whoever they pleased, no matter what their associations. She really wasn't arguing that point. Thirteen Stars had to be stopped. Their members had most certainly committed crimes. But when Sydney balanced those crimes against

the ones she had had to commit over the years—
breaking in and out of government facilities, high-
profile theft, threatening government officials—she
had a hard time feeling morally superior.

"Okay," Vaughn interrupted to set the meeting
back on track. "Whether or not we think Thirteen
Stars is working for the greater good, we can all
agree that they have been going outside of the law
to do that. Combined with the fact that they now
have part of the seismic bomb, I think we all further agree that we need to find out what they're
planning. The question is, how do we do that?"

"We can't just wait for them to make contact
with Sydney again," Nadia said.

"Cabot did leave me his business card with an
offer to join," Sydney suggested. "Maybe there's a
way to get in contact with him. Something we're
not seeing."

"I don't think that would work for our immedi-
ate purposes," Sloane said. "Cabot isn't going to
believe you just changed your mind and wanted to
go along with him because he asked. He thinks
you've already turned your back on the government
and everything it stands for. It will take a while to
build his trust. We do not have the luxury of time."

"So what do you suggest?" Sydney asked, honestly wondering what he had in mind.

"Thirteen Stars already thinks Sydney is working for a terrorist organization," Sloane said. "I suggest we convince them that they are right."

CHAPTER 15

VAN NUYS, CALIFORNIA

"Having a good afternoon?" Susan Piller asked when Cabot finally returned to the West Coast headquarters of Thirteen Stars. He knew she would be waiting for him, since she would have gotten back to the office an hour earlier. But he hadn't expected that she would be standing outside in front of his parking spot.

Cabot wondered how long she had been waiting there for him. Maybe she had a tracking device on *him*. It wasn't as though he had been out for a leisurely drive, though. He'd had to make sure he lost the tail.

"Got to see some crazy artwork, had a nice conversation with an old acquaintance, had a nice drive in the warm L.A. sun," Cabot replied. "I even considered putting the top down. Yeah, I'd say it was shaping up to be a nice day."

"You ditched the tail, I hope," Susan said as she followed him inside.

"No, they're right behind me," he said jokingly as he opened the door to the brick building and let her inside first.

The painted sign on the glass door read: FRANKLIN PRINT SHOP. It was located in the back of an industrial/business center off Roscoe Boulevard. Usually the building sat empty except for the rare times operatives from Thirteen Stars used it as the West Coast base of operations.

It was a typical Los Angeles–area office building with exposed heating ducts, a concrete slab of a floor, and metallic accents around the big open main room that housed a stylish cube farm surrounded by offices along the outer walls. Cabot had chosen it specifically because it was the polar opposite of the D.C. office, with its gray carpeting and traditional design of offices, hallways, and cubes all in a row.

As they walked past the empty reception desk into the bustling cube farm and office area, Cabot noted that the number of people in the space was an even rarer occurrence than usual. It was the first time the entire membership of Thirteen Stars was there at the same time.

The team was usually headquartered in D.C. That was where they had most of their phone taps and their impressive list of informants monitoring the global intelligence landscape for them. It was true that Thirteen Stars had only a dozen members on its active roster, but the group's resources stretched out quite far. It wasn't surprising, considering how many people were unhappy with the way things were being run in Washington.

"I still don't get why you needed to fly everyone out here on a moment's notice," Susan said as they walked through the busy operatives nodding hello. "We took care of Sprague and Martine. We have the bomb casing. We could have handled getting the core ourselves. Or with a minimal contingent."

"Not if Arvin Sloane is involved," Cabot said as he lowered his voice. "If he's the one pulling the strings on this, I'm afraid we don't have enough people on hand, no matter how good a team we are."

Susan eyed him suspiciously. She had been a stellar FBI analyst who was repeatedly passed over for promotion to field agent. To this day she still didn't know the reason she'd been held back was because her superior had taken an unprofessional liking to her and didn't want her to leave his office.

"Then why did we bring the bomb casing here?" she asked. "Shouldn't it be as far from Arvin Sloane as humanly possible?"

"Yes," Cabot admitted. "But if Sloane is in on this, I want to make sure the casing is as close to me as possible. I don't trust anyone else to keep it from that man."

Susan continued to look uncertain, but she let the matter rest. "Speaking of Sloane, we've been going through the CIA files. So far there's nothing we didn't know. Or at least suspect."

"I didn't think there would be," Cabot said. "But the important part is that we've got proof that the CIA knows all about his criminal past. When the world finds out that the head of Omnifan and the recipient of a UN honor is such an evil bastard and the CIA did *nothing* to punish him for his crimes . . . Well, I think Thirteen Stars will be able to initiate a positive change in the way intelligence is run in the United States."

Susan still looked skeptical, but she didn't challenge Cabot on his assertions. He appreciated that aspect of her personality. She knew when to challenge him and when to hold her tongue.

"I've left the files we've already gone over on your desk," Susan said as they reached his temporary office. "I'll keep you posted on the rest. There's a lot there. And it's some very . . . interesting reading. And video too."

"Sounds exciting," he joked as he stepped inside the office and closed the door behind him.

It had been a long couple of days. What had started out as a simple execution of an arms dealer had led to a much more involved plot that could actually lead him to finally getting revenge. So far it was only a guess that Sloane was involved, but Cabot knew the guy well enough to know that this smacked of his MO. Recruiting Sydney Bristow to work for him again was the kind of insidious criminal genius that Cabot couldn't help but respect and fear.

Cabot hadn't expected to cross paths with his old enemy on this mission. He'd known it would happen one day, he just hadn't thought that it would be today. Not that he had confirmation that Sloane was pulling the strings. But it fell into the criminal's usual agenda: betray a lesser criminal (namely, Sprague) in order to gain access to a powerful new ally (namely, Martine). It brought Cabot no small amount of satisfaction to know he had taken out two major players and put a crimp in Sloane's plans.

And even if Sloane *wasn't* involved with this particular crime. Even if he really had changed his ways. It didn't matter. Sloane still had past crimes to atone for. Sydney Bristow aside, Cabot had an opportunity to finally get to Arvin Sloane; he had Sloane's file. And it was time to act.

He moved to his desk and examined the files his operatives had obtained from the CIA. According to his tech guy, Reed, the computer system had been surprisingly easy to hack into. It was obvious they held only the basic archives on Sloane. The CIA might be lax nowadays, but they weren't incompetent. The good stuff had to be locked farther away from prying eyes. It didn't matter. A cursory glance at the partial file on his desk showed that he had enough to make Sloane's life difficult.

The Sydney Bristow aspect still bugged him, though. If she *had* turned her back on the government, it wasn't as though he didn't understand where she was coming from. She certainly wasn't the first operative to grow disillusioned by the CIA. He just hadn't expected her to turn so quickly. To go from CIA operative to making arms deals and attempting to ally herself with a weapons designer so quickly just felt wrong. Everything he knew about the agent made him believe that she would be one of the last to go bad.

He couldn't help but picture her face when he had met her at the museum. She obviously hadn't remembered him. It wasn't a surprise. They had only spoken briefly once, and she had been just four years old at the time.

Jack Bristow had had a small cocktail party in his house in Charleston. His wife, Laura Bristow, had warmly welcomed Cabot into their home. Being that he was the only single person in the small group, she had gone out of her way to make sure he felt included. At the time, the guests had thought that Laura was simply a schoolteacher who had no idea what her husband's job entailed. A few years later rumors spread about the truth behind that facade. Cabot wondered if that may have had something to do with Sydney's quick turn against the CIA.

During the course of the evening, little Sydney Bristow had come downstairs, using the classic wanting-a-glass-of-water routine to check out the party. Maybe it was because Cabot was the only one not obviously attached to a wife or date, but while her mother went to the kitchen, Sydney quickly attached herself to Cabot, asking him if he was having fun and why he was wearing such an ugly tie. As Laura returned with the water, Sydney had promised to make him a new tie for the next time he came to their house. Cabot had dismissed the offer shortly after Sydney returned to bed, but damned if Jack hadn't brought him a construction-paper tie from Sydney the following Monday.

It was hard to believe that Jack Bristow's little girl was possibly working for a terrorist like Sloane. Cabot knew he was jumping to conclusions, but he was really good at what he did. He couldn't count the number of times he had been right in developing far more intricate scenarios with less information than he had in this case.

Cabot wondered if he should alert Jack Bristow to

his daughter's activities, but he didn't even know where to begin. He hadn't spoken to Jack in a couple decades, but he doubted the man would be receptive to what Cabot had to say.

That was the only reason he hadn't killed her on the ship. He had only worked with Jack Bristow a handful of times back in D.C., but the man still impressed Cabot to this day. Bristow's intensity and his strict adherence to the CIA code back in the seventies had taught Cabot a lot about the kind of man he wanted to be.

Sure, they had lost touch. Cabot had heard about the series of tragedies that had rocked Bristow's world. Then there was the confusion back in the early nineties over the Alliance and SD-6. Cabot still wasn't sure what he'd almost stumbled into, but he did know that Jack was involved somehow.

It was possible that the Jack Bristow of today wasn't the same man he remembered. But Cabot wasn't about to add to the list of tragedies by killing the man's daughter.

He still held out hope for Sydney Bristow. She had only left the CIA a short time ago. It wasn't possible for her to be too deep into Sloane's organization yet. If, in fact, she was working for Sloane.

She had to be. No one else could have gotten to her that quickly. Maybe Sloane had been working at her all along. He just seized the opportunity when he saw he had his chance. Cabot hoped that he could steer her back. Offer her the kind of justice the CIA could not. And he really did like the symmetry of making her the thirteenth member of his little team.

"Hey," Susan said as she popped her head into his office without bothering to knock. "We've got something."

"In Sloane's file?" Cabot asked.

"Actually, yes," she said. "But that can wait. We've found something much more interesting."

"What?" he asked as he motioned for her to take a seat.

"Reed intercepted a communiqué," she said as she stepped into the office and sat in one of his guest chairs. "Sprague's men are going nuts trying to reorganize now that he, Martine, and two of his top guys are out of the picture thanks to us."

"Always good to know your work is paying off," Cabot said feeling a proper amount of job satisfaction. "Now we can go in and start shutting down some warehouses."

"Yeah," Susan said. "But it gets better. Or worse, depending on how you look at it."

"How I look at what?"

"Like I said, Reed hacked into their communications system again," Susan explained. She was referring to the technical genius Cabot had recruited right out of the CIA academy. The young buck proved that it didn't always take years of servitude to develop a good case of jadedness. "He found correspondence from a woman claiming to be waiting for her shipment of Scorpion Pistols."

"Sydney Bristow," Cabot surmised. "But she knows Sprague is dead. I also told her we intercepted the shipment."

"Yes," Susan said. "With all the turmoil in the organization, a new guy has risen to the top overnight. A guy named Telasco. We think he was the one in charge of Martine's security."

"Doesn't that just give you high hopes for the organization," Cabot mocked. "Considering how well he did on his last assignment."

"Anyway, he informed Bristow of Sprague's death and the missing pistols," Susan continued. "And that's where it gets interesting."

"I get the feeling I'm not going to like this," Cabot said.

"Oh, you're going to hate it," she confirmed. "She starts playing the guy and taking credit for our work. She told Telasco that her order for the Scorpion Pistols was a setup. That *she* was behind the hit on Sprague, the raid on Martine's lab, *and* the raid on the warehouse. She's using the information to structure another deal."

Cabot did not like where this was going. "How?"

"She told Telasco that she has the seismic bomb. Both the core and the outer casing," Susan said. "But she hasn't figured out how to use it. You know how Martine was obsessively anal about her work. Nothing in the files is complete. She keeps things like the core and the casing apart so no one can get at both easily. Well, it looks like Bristow figured out how things worked. She was fishing around for information, and she got the mother lode."

Cabot sat straight up. This was definitely not good. "This the 'better' news? 'Cause the way I look at it, things just got worse."

"Hold on," she said. "Telasco was more than

willing to deal with Bristow. Whatever information he has is useless if she's got the bomb, right? So he offered to give her what she wanted."

"Which is?"

"A disc," Susan replied. "A disc with information on how to operate the bomb. Reed thinks that the information he pulled from Martine's computer combined with whatever is on the disc . . . He thinks someone with half a brain could make their own casing."

"And by 'half a brain' Reed means a Mensa-size genius," Cabot guessed.

"Well, yeah," Susan admitted. "But I gotta tell you, I was watching Reed hack into Martine's computer on the *Triton*. You know, when Bristow's people were already on it. Reed threw everything he could at those guys, and they managed to fight him off. Probably even salvaged some of the files, too. I think Bristow's got more than half a brain working for her."

"You mean Sloane," Cabot seethed.

"Sloane or whoever," Susan said. "Either way, pretty soon they're going to have a damn powerful bomb. I can't believe this Telasco guy would just sell it away that easily."

"A deal this size would be a great way to launch himself into the business," Cabot said. "And not just him. This kind of thing would make a name for everyone involved. And not a good one."

If Sydney Bristow did work for Sloane, Cabot had just gotten about the worst piece of information he could imagine ever receiving. The things that Sloane could do with that bomb were horrifying. It would be a heck of a way to get back in on the global terrorism scene.

"When's the meet?" Cabot asked.

"Tomorrow morning," Susan replied. "At the train yards by Union Station."

"It's here? In L.A?"

"The first piece of good news," Susan acknowledged.

Cabot leaned back in his seat and considered the situation. Suddenly it seemed a lot less horrifying.

"You don't seem too thrilled," she said. "That's the good news."

"That the key to stopping another seismic bomb just dropped in our laps?" Cabot asked. "It's a trap."

"Maybe," Susan admitted. "But we can't just

ignore it. Whoever that Bristow woman is working for has the bomb's core. She's halfway there. If the intel is real, we have to act on it. There's too much risk otherwise."

"You're right," Cabot said as he glanced at his desk calendar. "Doesn't mean I like it, though. Let me guess, the shipment is coming in at eight in the morning."

"Seven thirty," Susan said with a small amount of awe mixed with suspicion. "How'd you do that?"

Cabot looked at the picture sitting on his desk beside the calendar. Since it was a temporary office, he didn't usually bring knickknacks or personal items to decorate it. He especially didn't like anything that could lead back to him in case the place were compromised. But this was different.

He carried this picture wherever he went. It was an image of Kyle. His former partner at the CIA. Whenever Cabot was worried that he was getting in too deep, he looked at the picture and remembered why he had gotten into the vigilante business in the first place.

Now he finally had the opportunity to avenge his partner's death. There wasn't a chance in hell he was going to pass it up.

"Cabot?" Susan prompted. He wasn't surprised to realize that he had drifted off for a moment. It was happening more and more these days. Ever since he'd formed Thirteen Stars, his mind would wander back to the motivation for the cause.

"Arvin Sloane is speaking to his little pet-project organization at eight," Cabot explained. "Seems like the perfect cover for him. He couldn't possibly be involved in the exchange since he'll be being broadcast to a global audience at the same time."

"So are we going in or aren't we?" Susan asked.

"Oh, we're going in," Cabot said. "Just not the way Sloane is expecting."

CHAPTER 16

LOS ANGELES CONVENTION CENTER

Arvin Sloane paced the floor of the West Hall of the L.A. Convention Center. There were over three thousand Omnifam employees milling about, enjoying their buffet breakfast and waiting for his speech announcing all of the company's initiatives for the coming year. People had flown in from all over the country—and different parts of the world—for the meeting. It was also being sent out via video to Omnifam offices around the globe. It was a ridiculous expenditure for a nonprofit organization, but Sloane understood the power of PR more than most.

"Teams are in place," Jack reported via cell phone. "We're just waiting for Thirteen Stars to make its move."

Sloane wasn't nervous about the speech at all. He was annoyed that he'd been forced to be out of the office at a time when he was most needed. He didn't doubt that his team was more than capable of handling the current mission on their own. No, mission success was not his concern. The thing that bothered him was that they were still new to working together in the current configuration. This wasn't the time to be dealing with a vigilante organization that could blur the lines of his objectives for APO.

"I want to be updated every five minutes," Sloane said back to Jack. An annoying production assistant was buzzing around him trying to get his attention.

"Are you planning on taking my calls in the middle of your speech?" Jack asked with that damnable cocky attitude he came out with from time to time. "I'll call in when there is something to report. Until then, why don't you enjoy your moment in the spotlight."

"Excuse me, Mr. Sloane?" the production assistant attempted to interrupt.

"I don't give a damn about this presentation," Sloane said into the phone as he waved off the annoying peon. "This is a complicated matter. I don't like being out of the loop."

"Our team excels at complicated matters," Jack reminded him. "There is nothing to worry about. However, you are keeping me from overseeing the operation. So, if there's nothing else . . ."

Sloane considered his response. He knew there was nothing he could do from the convention center. He'd be even less available once he was on the dais. Jack was more than capable of overseeing the mission. Sloane just didn't want to have to wait until it was over to know that it was successful. APO had only been in existence for a short time. He didn't need some upstart organization like Thirteen Stars putting his group in jeopardy.

"Call me when the team gets the go-ahead," Sloane said as he closed his cell phone. He looked over to Nadia standing off to the side, trying to not get in the way. He wished he could just enjoy this time with her as he prepared to make his speech, but current events were conspiring to keep that from happening.

Aside from the mission ops under way, the

production team in charge of transmitting the conference was running into all sorts of problems with the feed, ranging from serious issues to inane. At last update they had managed to connect the global closed-circuit system. So it was at least possible that his speech would go out to the foreign offices. He really wished he could have Marshall stop in for five minutes and show these people how to do their jobs.

"Mr. Sloane?" The production assistant came up to him the moment he ended the call. He was a nervous young man who had introduced himself as Shawn or Don or something similar. "I'm sorry to bother you, but we've got another problem."

"What is it this time?" Sloane asked with exasperation. If he were still in charge of Omnifam, this whole production would have run considerably smoother.

"It's your tie, sir," the production assistant said. "We ran some camera tests. The tie bleeds on-screen."

Sloane looked down at his red and white striped tie. Emily had bought it for him. She had purchased most of his ties, actually. He had only bought a few on his own in the years since her death, and his wardrobe was soon going to be in need of a considerable update.

"And what do you propose we do about it?" Sloane asked. It wasn't as though he had an overly sentimental attachment to his ties or anything, even though they had been gifts from his late wife. He didn't *need* to be wearing this exact tie for the presentation. He simply hadn't thought to bring any other ties with him when he got dressed that morning.

"We've actually got a selection," the production assistant said as he scurried over to a table and came back with a variety of ties. "We ran tests on all of them. It would be best if you stayed in the gray-to-blue spectrum."

"Fine," Sloane said as he grabbed the nearest tie. "Thank you," he added dismissively.

It took the production assistant a moment to realize he was being dismissed. Once the dawn came, the kid apologized again for bothering him and made a hasty exit. It was likely there were some more people he could annoy in the building.

Sloane pulled off his "bleeding" red tie as he walked over to Nadia. They were in the greenroom area off to the side of backstage. He had walked the convention floor earlier to get a feel for the space. It was a slight overkill to host the event in the convention center, since any large hotel would have done fine. As it was, the temporary wall between halls A and B had to be closed off so the space wasn't overwhelmingly empty.

Thirty-five hundred chairs—mostly full now— sat in rows on the other side of the curtain. The dais had a row of chairs where Sloane, the Omnifam executives, and other honored officials would sit. There had been talk of inviting the president, but apparently he had declined the invitation. Sloane assumed that someone on the president's staff had suggested that he shouldn't share a stage with a man who was once considered a terrorist, even though they had met before on several occasions when cameras weren't around. Sloane found that part of the hypocrisy rather annoying, but he was used to it by now.

"There seems to be a problem with my tie," Sloane said when he reached Nadia. "Would you be so kind as to hold it for me?"

"Sure," she said as she took his tie and carefully rolled it up and put it in her bag.

Sloane proceeded to tie the one lent to him by

the production assistant. "I'm so glad you could still join me this morning," he said. "It will be nice to see your face in the audience when I make my speech. I've never spoken to such a large audience before."

"I know you wanted me here," Nadia said. "And I'm glad I can be here for you. Though I can't help but think I should be on the mission too."

"Sydney suggested the same thing," Sloane replied as he finished with the tie. "I have total faith that the rest of the team can handle it. I'd much rather have you by my side this morning. Now . . . how do I look?"

Nadia stepped up to him and adjusted his tie. "Quite presentable," she said. It was one of the few father-daughter moments they had experienced. But it was over too soon for Sloane. As she stepped away, he grabbed her hand and held her close to him for a moment.

"I really am glad you decided to come," he said genuinely.

"Me too," she agreed, after a slight hesitation. He knew that she had wanted Sydney to come along as well. Nadia still wasn't comfortable spending time with him one-on-one. He understood. Especially considering what had happened between them in Siena. But the mission provided Sydney with an excuse to bow out at the last second.

Sloane wished he could have bowed out himself. He would much rather have been at APO instead of at this early-morning dog and pony show. But for the plan to work he needed to be making a high-profile appearance, to avoid any possible links between him and Sydney and the U.S. government.

On the personal side, he also knew that events like this were important to show Nadia and the world that he had changed. It was a difficult balance. His work at APO was just as important, if not more so. And this latest mission had taken a decidedly personal turn.

Chase had forwarded the files that had been accessed by Thirteen Stars so he knew what they would be dealing with. There was nothing too surprising in the archived records. The results from Jack and Sydney's investigations into SD-6, some old money trails, and grainy surveillance video didn't worry him. It was certainly nothing that Thirteen Stars couldn't have found out from other sources.

Sloane's main concern was that they were

looking at his files in the first place. If they had already linked Sydney to him, how soon before they found out about APO?

Sloane had known that his appointment as the head of the division would cause some concerns. He was dealing with them on a daily basis. But he could handle the internal problems. Sydney, Dixon, and Jack were his biggest challenges, but he was working on them. If his involvement with APO got out, he wasn't sure that even he could spin that story.

"Is your mind on the mission?" Nadia asked softly, so that none of the backstage personnel could hear.

"In a way," Sloane admitted. "I am thinking about Thirteen Stars. Their goal is noble, but their methods are misguided."

"Have you thought about bringing them in?" Nadia asked. "If they're all former FBI and CIA, maybe they could work for us. Instead of arresting them."

"Cabot would never work for me," Sloane said.

"But the rest of them," Nadia suggested. "They're just trying to do some good."

"Odd how we define 'good' by the *types* of assassinations they've carried out," Sloane said a little more harshly than he had intended. "I'm sorry, Nadia. But I've found that once an agent goes rogue, there is little chance of bringing him back. It's very hard to change."

"You managed," Nadia reminded him. "And I'd say you had more of a dramatic change to make."

"All the better for me to understand how difficult it is," Sloane said. "I know it's hypocritical of me to say this, but we can't reward Thirteen Stars for acting outside the law."

"Um . . . Mr. Sloane . . . ," the fidgety production assistant interrupted again. "I just wanted to give you the half-hour call. We've fixed all the glitches in the satellite broadcast, so we should be able to start promptly at eight."

"That is good news," Sloane said, turning on the charm. "And how is this new tie?"

"It looks great, sir," the PA replied. "And . . . can I just . . . I'd like to tell you what an honor it is to meet you. I've read all about the things you did with Omnifam before you stepped down. And I have to say, you are a true inspiration."

"Thank you," Sloane said. He meant it too. That little display was exactly why he had asked Nadia along on this excursion.

He could see that his daughter was having a hard time buying the sentiment, but he knew that the more Nadia heard people sing his praises, the more she would be receptive to them. He was actually glad that Sydney hadn't been able to come along this morning. She surely would have had a snide comment or an exaggerated eye roll to fill in the silence after the production assistant left.

"Do you want me to leave you alone so you can go over your speech?" Nadia asked.

"No," Sloane replied. "I'd much rather spend this time waiting with you."

CHAPTER 17

UNION STATION
LOS ANGELES

It began with a meet and it ends with a meet, Sydney thought as she checked her blond wig in the mirror. It wasn't an exact duplicate of the last one, but it was close enough. It didn't really matter, though. She didn't need to re-create herself exactly as she had appeared back in Bern. Everyone who had been involved in that meeting was now dead. And the one uninvited guest in Bern already knew that her old wig was somewhere in the Pacific. She just hoped that Cabot intended to show up this morning as well.

The change in wigs wasn't the only difference between the two meets. This time Sydney was much warmer, sitting in the heated interior of the car. It was still cool outside for an early L.A. morning, but definitely not the bone-chilling cold that she had experienced in Switzerland only a couple days before. And, of course, there was no crazy fountain of an ogre devouring children in the middle of the train yards.

The other difference was that Vaughn wasn't the only guardian angel watching over her at the moment. She couldn't see him in his position fifty yards away, but she knew he was there, along with Marshall and an APO strike team scattered about the yards.

Her father had arranged with Union Station security so that they had complete and sole access to the area. Of course, security didn't know anything about them being agents of a black ops team. Jack had sold security the story that he was the head of a DEA team trying to trap drug smugglers who had been using trains to ship their cargo around the country.

There was one other *major* difference between this meet and the first. This one was entirely bogus. Whereas the last one was only *partially* bogus.

With Maximilian Sprague's organization in disarray, it was simple for Marshall to hack into the communications system they had used to set up the original meet with Sprague in Bern. He then provided both ends of the e-mail correspondence between Lilia Von Malkin and the expected new leader of Sprague's organization.

It took only a minimal amount of research to determine that Dominic Telasco—the guard who had been in charge of Martine's detail—was the logical choice to head up the business. Sydney wondered if the original Telasco was still locked in the supply closet on the *Triton*.

Once Marshall had that information, it was just a matter of creating the e-mail chain in which Von Malkin and Telasco structured a deal for additional information on the seismic bomb. There was no actual disc, just as there was no actual Telasco on the other end of the communiqué. The whole setup was simply so that Thirteen Stars could hack into Marshall's hack and get the false information. Once that had happened, APO set their plan in motion.

Marshall had tried to secretly back-trace the hack

to get a location on Thirteen Stars' headquarters, but whoever they had doing their tech was too good for such an easy trace. It was no real surprise, since Marshall had gotten a taste of the guy's work when he "adapted" the Second-Skin technology.

And that was how Sydney found herself sitting seemingly alone in the train yards first thing in the morning waiting for Telasco—or a reasonable facsimile—to arrive.

"We're sending him in," Vaughn spoke through the communicator in Sydney's ear. She nodded almost imperceptibly to confirm she'd received the message, knowing he would pick up the movement through his high-powered binoculars. She didn't want to risk responding verbally, fearing that APO operatives weren't the only ones that had her under audio and visual surveillance at the moment.

Sydney saw the sedan drive around the abandoned train on her right and over the railroad tracks. The car pulled into the corridor between the two sets of trains where Sydney was waiting. The spot had been specifically chosen to minimize traffic. Each of the train cars was tightly sealed and alarmed so that no one could enter without being detected. There were only two angles of approach, and considering the height of the train cars, there were only two spots in the surrounding buildings from which someone could watch the meet.

Vaughn and Marshall were currently in one of those spots, in a seemingly sealed building on Sydney's right. The other spot was in an easily accessible building on her left. There was no guarantee that Thirteen Stars would use that building to watch the proceedings, but it was the logical choice.

Sydney waited as the sedan slowed to a stop at the prearranged distance. In keeping with the facade of the meet between two highly suspicious people, Marshall had set up very specific protocols for the arrival. Lilia Von Malkin would arrive first and wait for Dominic Telasco to appear. She would stay in her vehicle until Telasco's car came to a stop. Then they would both get out of their respective cars at the same time. It seemed like a pointless protocol since it wasn't an actual meet, but they were trying to sell it to Thirteen Stars' operatives as if it were real.

Considering that Telasco supposedly believed he was meeting with the person who had murdered his boss and Martine, and single-handedly destroyed their weapons trade, it made sense that security would be a concern. At the same time, APO didn't want to make it too difficult for Thirteen Stars to get involved. So Von Malkin and Telasco "agreed" that the meet would take place only between the two participants.

Once the car stopped, Sydney exited her vehicle at the same time Weiss exited the sedan. He was dressed similarly to how Telasco had been outfitted when Sydney met him on the *Triton*. He even sported a closely shaven fake beard. Vaughn had taken particular pleasure in seeing Weiss in it, which had everything to do with the earlier hard time Vaughn had gotten over his wig.

Sydney and Weiss slowly covered the distance between the two vehicles, making a show of being extremely aware of their surroundings. They needed to sell the performance as two untrusting participants.

"Ms. Van Malkin," Weiss said in character as they reached each other.

"It's *Von* Malkin," she corrected him, stopping a few feet away. They specifically did not shake hands or move too close to one another, trying to keep up the pretense of suspicion.

"Sorry," Weiss said. "Have to say it's rather rude of me to forget the name of the woman who arranged for my promotion."

"Some promotion," she said. "Do you even have a business left with Martine gone?"

"That was a difficult blow," Weiss said. He was speaking far more than the actual Telasco would have, but it was necessary that they have a detailed conversation for the plan to work. "But we've got more than enough stock to see out the year. And you don't think Sprague had all of his eggs in that particular basket. I inherited a rather nice network. I look forward to continued business with you."

"Let's not get ahead of ourselves," Sydney said. "One deal at a time."

"We have a visual on a pair of operatives from Thirteen Stars," Vaughn said over the comm. "Merlin's going to need a minute to pick up on audio. Keep the conversation going."

"I take it you've brought the information on the seismic bomb," Sydney said as previously scripted. "Please tell me that you have it on your person and you're not going to make this difficult."

"You must be kidding," Weiss said, playing up his role. "Do you think I would come to meet you with the disc on me? Or even nearby, for that matter? You've killed how many key members in my organization? Let's just say the disc is in the area. Once we finalize the deal, I will provide its location. I have no intention of being next on your hit list."

"We've got audio," Marshall said a little too loudly over the comm. He was so excitable when he got to experience his technology working in the field. "It's going to take some time before I can back-trace the communications, so keep talking. The next voice you hear will be that of a member of Thirteen Stars."

"I understand your concern," Sydney said, confirming she'd received Marshall's message while remaining in character. "But I assure you I was only doing what I felt needed to be done to ensure the best deal for myself. I think you will offer me a better price than your former employer would have."

"Can you believe this woman?" an unfamiliar male voice said through the comm. "Taking credit for Cabot's work. If she would move a few more feet into the open, I'd be happy to shut her up. I'd even let her take credit for that one too."

Sydney made a mental note to stay fixed in her spot. She doubted that anyone was going to fire on her until they found out the location of the disc. Neither she nor Weiss had any intention of allowing that piece of information to come up during their discussion. Aside from the fact that it was the only thing the Thirteen Stars operatives had come for, they weren't going to say anything simply because the disc didn't exist.

At least the voice confirmed that they had both visual and audio on her and Weiss. That would help Marshall with the second part of the plan. It had been a calculated risk, but they figured Cabot's organization probably followed CIA protocols. Sydney didn't want to think about what would happen if Thirteen Stars didn't do things by the book. If that was the case, this entire charade was a waste of time.

"Well, I've got the pudgy guy," another voice said.

Sydney knew they couldn't react, but she could see that Weiss was offended. "Pudgy?" he mouthed incredulously. She did her best to stay in character so that she wouldn't laugh.

"I understand why you think I'd be willing to

deal," Weiss said after his momentary slip out of character. "But, considering the bomb is just as useless to you as the disc is to me, you shouldn't expect too much of a bargain."

"I wish they'd just cut to the chase," one of the voices said in Sydney's ear. Neither of the voices they'd heard so far belonged to Harrison Cabot. The plan would still work if he wasn't around, but she didn't like the possibility that he could be somewhere else at the moment.

"Cut the chatter," a third voice said. It wasn't as clear as the other two voices, but Sydney could tell it definitely belonged to a female. She suspected that it might belong to the woman Dixon had fought with on the *Triton*.

"Sorry, base ops," one of the voices said.

"Gotcha," Marshall's voice came over the comm. It almost sounded like Marshall was talking to the other guys, but the APO team were the only ones that could hear his voice. They were on two different comm signals. "Need to triangulate the location. Keep 'em talking."

Sydney and Weiss had prepared for that request. She figured Marshall's job would be much easier because they seemed to have a chatty bunch around them. She couldn't help but wonder why Cabot hadn't spoken up yet, though.

"Just one question," Weiss said, baiting the trap. "How did you manage to find the location of the warehouse so quickly after you stole Martine's computer files? I know for a fact that information was encrypted. *Well* encrypted."

APO did know that for a fact too, since Marshall's tech assistant (whom Weiss had nicknamed Mini-Marshall) had managed to retrieve the warehouse locator from Martine's damaged files. He was having a difficult time decrypting it himself, but Marshall had devised it as a test for the kid. Since they had other more pressing issues at the moment, Sloane hadn't minded the delay.

"Child's play." Sydney laughed. "Any idiot could have figured it out."

"That's it," the first voice said angrily. "If I get a shot, I'm taking it."

"Negative," the female voice from base ops said.

Sydney knew they'd need more for Marshall to triangulate the location of base ops. She wasn't exactly clear how his listening device could tap into the Thirteen Stars communication system and provide the coordinates of the source of the transmission, but that didn't matter. The only important part that Marshall had told her was that he needed to keep a constant connection between the operatives and their headquarters to get the location.

That made her next action clear. Weiss knew it too. And his eyes were silently pleading with Sydney not to risk it.

"Don't be mad," she said tauntingly to Weiss/Telasco and the eavesdropping operatives. "My people are very good. You didn't have a chance at keeping it secret." Then she took a couple steps in the direction of what she assumed to be the operatives' line of sight.

"Just a few more steps, honey," the man said into her ear.

"Stand down," the woman from base ops said. "That's an order."

"But, Susan, she's taking credit for Reed's work," the guy insisted. "That little guy slaves over the computer all day and night. And this woman is acting like it's child's play. I think she's asking for it."

"Do you think I care who gets credit for what?" the woman—Susan—asked. "Reed's a big boy. Not some stupid glory hound. And he'd say the same thing. Now grow up. All we need is the location of the disc. Then you can do whatever you want with her."

"How 'bout we shoot her, then follow the pudgy guy back to the disc?" the other on-site operative asked.

"Almost there," Marshall said.

Sydney was trying to focus on her job, but it was difficult with all the voices in her head at the moment. She took another step into the open.

"Carter. Rossi," Susan said in a severe tone. "Do not make me contact Cabot. Do as you were instructed."

"Got it!" Marshall said. "I've got the location of Thirteen Stars' headquarters."

"Relay the information to Dixon," Vaughn ordered over the comm. "Everyone else, move in. Move in!"

Sydney took two steps *out* of the line of fire and continued her conversation. "Now, can we get down to business?"

"Certainly," Weiss said.

On cue, a half-dozen masked agents came barreling out of the side building toward Sydney and Weiss, screaming, "Freeze! FBI! Get down! Get down!"

They fell to the ground as instructed. It was all

part of the plan. If Cabot wanted to believe Sydney Bristow had gone rogue, APO wanted him to think her foray into the criminal life hadn't lasted long.

"Damn!" the voices in her ear said.

"The Feds are here!" the first voice said. "They're all over the place."

Sydney didn't think a half dozen qualified as "all over the place," but she wasn't about to start a discussion on semantics. She was too busy looking shocked while lying facedown on the ground.

"They're arresting Sydney Bristow and Telasco," the second voice reported. It sounded to Sydney like they were packing up their equipment.

"Abort!" Susan yelled over the comm. "Abort!"

At that point the communications intercept cut off, but Sydney didn't need to hear it to know what was going on. The APO strike force confirmed they had the operatives in custody a couple minutes later. As the audio had suggested, there were only two operatives on-site. The rest of the team must have been back at headquarters, and Marshall had already relayed those coordinates to Dixon.

The only question that remained was whether or not Harrison Cabot was there as well.

CHAPTER 18

VAN NUYS, CALIFORNIA

"They gave of themselves for the greater good," Susan Piller spoke in a formal tone as she laid her headset on the table. She knew that it sounded pretentious. It had sounded pretentious when Cabot said it over the phone to her a couple seconds ago. But they *had* just lost two of their members.

True, Carter and Rossi weren't dead, but they also weren't going to be enjoying their freedom for a while. The government had a way of punishing those who were perceived as betraying the country.

Susan would have laughed at the hypocrisy of the notion if it weren't so frighteningly true. If only the government could understand what Thirteen Stars was working for, then they wouldn't need to be in business.

"What's with the sermonizing?" former FBI agent/hotshot Peter Willoughby asked. After Reed he was the youngest member of the team. At times Reed seemed far older than he did. In fact, Reed seemed far older than most of their operatives, especially Carter and Rossi.

"Our agents deserve a moment of our respect for martyring themselves for the cause," Susan said. She didn't really feel the captured men had even come close to earning that respect. Particularly in light of their behavior on the current mission. But Cabot had taught her that half their job was about perception. If the rest of the team perceived the nobility of the cause, they would be more willing to work for the good of their overall mission.

Carter and Rossi had been screwups since they'd joined the cause over a year before. Both men were in their late thirties, and they acted like they were *half* Reed's age. Susan suspected that

Cabot had suggested they volunteer for the mission because he wanted to be rid of them as much as she did. Not that she was ever going to ask Cabot about it. It wasn't a good idea to suggest that he was doing anything even remotely underhanded. He took his moral high ground *very* seriously.

"I still don't get why they did it," Pete said. "They went in knowing it was a trap."

"Don't know that for sure," Susan said. "Sounded like Sydney Bristow was taken by surprise as well. Could've been an act, but either way, the disc, the core, and the casing are in three different places. Seems like our work here is done."

Susan hoped that was the case. If Bristow turned over the core to the seismic bomb and the Feds managed to get the instruction disc, she didn't want to think about what they would do with it. She used to be in the FBI. She knew they couldn't be trusted.

"Yeah, but there was a good chance it *was* a trap," Pete insisted. "At least that's what we thought going in. If they—"

"Hold it," Susan said, putting up a hand for emphasis. "If you think this is the part where we have some big discussion about the ideology of our work and how we're going for the 'greater good' and all that, save it for Cabot. I'm just in this for the health benefits."

"You get benefits?" Pete asked jokingly. "Man, I knew I needed to negotiate a better contract. Next thing you're going to tell me is you get paid sick leave, too."

The rest of the team laughed at the joke. They had stayed quiet during the exchange. Susan hoped that meant they all understood the motivation behind the mission and why it had been necessary to put Carter and Rossi in the line of fire.

Either that or the group just didn't care enough to question it. At times Susan wondered about Cabot's hiring practices. He said that he only brought in people who understood his cause, but Susan thought most of the team was a little more mercenary than Cabot had intended. Aside from Reed, she really didn't care for most of them.

"We'll make a list of contract demands," Susan joked. "I think it's time we started a union." She ignored the sound of the approaching helicopter. The office was fairly close to the Van Nuys airport, and they heard air traffic throughout the day.

"So what do we do now?" Pete said. "Just sit

around and wait for Cabot and Reed to report in?"

"It's a shame we don't have a TV in here," Jean Graham, former NSA agent, commented. "I figure our boys might be making the news soon."

"Let's hope they just *make* news," Pete added. "I don't think we want them to show up *on* the news."

"No," Susan conceded, raising her voice to be heard over the rising din. "That wouldn't be good at all."

The helicopter seemed to be hovering in one place. She figured there must have been an accident on the 405. Whenever traffic backed up, all the local stations sent in the air support so they'd have nice pretty pictures of the cars all lined up going nowhere. She had already seen three helicopter groupings fill the air since they'd arrived at the L.A. satellite office a couple days before.

"What the hell is going on?" Susan asked.

The helicopter sounded like it was about to land on the ceiling. Then it dawned on her that it *was* about to land. Or someone was.

"Wipe the computers!" Susan ordered. "Now!"

She watched for a moment as the team sprung into action. Pete went for the mainframe and started pulling drives. Jean severed all links with the office back in D.C. No one was there at the moment, but the files at main headquarters were invaluable for their future work. The rest of the team worked to disable their personal computers and laptops. Susan hoped that someone would have the sense to go into Cabot's office and do the same.

"Once everything's wiped, get out of here!" Susan yelled from her office. She hit the kill switch on her computer, but didn't watch to confirm the hard drive was wiped. She grabbed her gun and ran for the back exit. There was something far more important that she had to do.

"Where are you going?" Pete hollered after her.

Susan didn't have time to answer. She heard glass smashing as a black-clad strike force came crashing through the windows. She could tell by the ropes that some of them were dropping in directly from the helicopter. Pieces of glass flew behind her as she exited the main room and dashed down a small corridor to the back exit.

She could hear gunfire and hoped it was her team doing the firing. She wasn't sure who was attacking or how they had found the headquarters, but that didn't matter at the moment. She had to get to the storage room.

Susan burst through the back door and almost ran right into an operative. Even with the unexpected shock of seeing him, she managed to draw her gun before he could. Her shot was wild, but she clipped him in the shoulder, sending him to the ground as she ran past. She didn't bother firing a second shot at the man. There wasn't time to slow down and do the job right.

The helicopter was at the front of the building, so she managed to avoid the wind from its rotors, but she could not get away from the sound. There was still about an hour before the industrial park began to come to life with workers. She was glad that there was no one to get in the way. This would definitely have attracted unwanted attention.

"FBI! Freeze!" a man yelled behind her. Susan didn't care. She kept running, shifting to a serpentine route that she had learned back when she had her FBI training. The irony wasn't lost on her as she approached the back building.

Susan realized only a few yards before she reached the glass doors that she didn't have the keys on her. Even if she'd had them with her, there probably wouldn't have been time to unlock the door. The FBI agent was right behind her.

She raised her gun and began firing on the door. Glass imploded as she pushed her way through to the inside. There was glass in her hair and on her clothes, but as long as she wasn't bleeding and could still run, it didn't matter.

She ran past the unoccupied offices of the shell building. It had seemed like such an unnecessary expense when Cabot bought it. A building to constantly sit unoccupied near the L.A. branch office that itself spent most of the year unoccupied. A "backup" he had called it, with a money trail entirely different from the main building.

A glorified storage unit was what Susan had called it. But now she was just glad that it was close by.

Susan ran into the kitchen and opened the bottom cabinet. Cabot had said it would be the last place anyone would look. He hadn't even bothered to put a lock on the cabinet because he didn't want to call attention to it.

The box was right where they had left it. On the outside it read: COFFEE CUPS. But inside there was something with a bit more of a jolt to it.

Susan pulled the seismic bomb casing out of the box. She could hear the FBI agent carefully making his way through the building. She knew that any noise would draw him right to her, but she had no choice. Whether or not the guy was really with the FBI, Susan couldn't risk letting the bomb casing fall into the wrong hands.

As far as she was concerned, the "wrong hands" was defined as anyone who was not a member of Thirteen Stars.

She lifted the metal casing by one of the handles on its sides. The design was truly impressive, and she didn't usually notice those kinds of things. It looked like a giant silver pill. It was smooth on the outside, save for the copper handle on either side. The interior, as Reed had shown her, was a mass of circuitry and wiring that Susan would never understand.

But that didn't matter anymore. In a moment it would be dust.

The prior residents of the empty building had upgraded the place to look far better than it needed to for being in the back end of an industrial park. Susan figured the last owner had been one of those trendy dot-com businesses that went crazy with the spending until the company went bust. As such, the kitchen was a work of art with tile flooring and granite countertops.

Susan placed her gun in her belt. Though it seemed ridiculous to be unarmed at the moment, she couldn't do what needed to be done with the gun in her hand. Once the gun was secure, she lifted the bomb casing above her head, using both of the copper handles. Cabot wouldn't have liked what she was about to do, but there was no choice.

Susan closed her eyes and slammed the seismic bomb casing into the countertop.

She could hear the agent's footsteps approaching quickly as she slammed the device into the granite again and again. She opened her eyes to check the progress and was gratified by what she saw. The previous owners had obviously gotten their money's worth. The device was dented and bleeding circuitry. The granite wasn't even scratched.

"Don't move!" the agent said from the door. The voice was vaguely familiar, but she couldn't place it.

Susan turned to see that the masked agent had his gun aimed right at her chest. The bomb casing was pretty much destroyed, but she needed to make sure that it was unsalvageable. Another good blow against the granite should do it.

If the guy *was* with the FBI, he wouldn't shoot her unless she went for her gun or made a move in his direction. Of course, if he wasn't a Fed, he'd kill her if she so much as flinched. But Susan didn't care. She had a responsibility to Thirteen Stars.

She had a responsibility to herself.

Susan closed her eyes again and said a little prayer. It was funny to her how even a lapsed Catholic like herself found God in moments like this. Not that she had many moments like this in her life to compare it to.

Letting out a howl, she slammed the casing into the granite one last time.

She didn't hear the shot fired, but she felt the bullet rip into her skin. She had never been shot before. It didn't feel like she thought it would. It was more of a pinprick than a gaping hole. But the results were the same. She opened her eyes to see the agent still standing in the doorway.

Then everything went dark.

Dixon made sure the woman was secured to the chair, like the rest of her team. Eight former federal officers in custody for crimes that, up until yesterday, no one had really sought them out for. Having come close to the edge himself a few times over the past several years, he knew what they felt, but would never understand how they could turn their backs on the government in the way that they had.

"Change often comes from the inside," he mumbled to the woman he had sedated and carried back to the main building.

She had destroyed the casing for the seismic bomb. He didn't need Marshall to examine it to tell him that. Circuit boards were smashed. Wires were severed and hanging loosely in all directions. Even with Stefani Martine's partial files, he doubted that it could be rebuilt.

To be honest, he didn't mind at all. If anything, he was glad the woman had destroyed it. Saved him from worrying about what would happen after he turned it over to Sloane. But still, he had a job to do and he had to get started.

Dixon could have begun the interrogation with any of the members. His squad had tranqued all eight of them, and they were resting comfortably in their chairs. The strike team had only suffered one minor injury. The rest of the team's vests had protected them from the bullets fired by the Thirteen Stars operatives.

This woman seemed to be Cabot's second in command. She was the one who had gone for the bomb casing. She was the one who had fought him on the ship. It stood to reason that she'd be the toughest in the group to crack, but she'd also have the most useful information.

Dixon took the capsule out of the pocket of his vest. He held it under the woman's nose and cracked it open. Once the stench hit her nostrils, she abruptly threw back her head and came out of her stupor.

"Whoa!" she said as she regained her focus. "Thought I was dead there for a moment. Glad you turned out to be who you said you are."

Dixon didn't bother to correct her. If she wanted to believe that he was actually with the FBI, that was fine with him. She was going to be transferred to the real FBI soon enough, anyway. He had kept his mask on so that she wouldn't recognize him from the *Triton*. The last thing they needed was to link the FBI to him and Sydney. That would certainly raise some unwanted questions.

"Where is Cabot?" Dixon asked. He threw a nasal affectation into his voice so she wouldn't recognize it from their fight on the *Triton*. "And the other one?"

"The other one?" the woman stalled as she turned to look at her sleeping operatives. "What other one?"

"I believe his name is Reed," Dixon said, taking a chance with the information Marshall had provided. The woman tried not to react, but he could see in her eyes that he had guessed correctly.

Dixon knew no one had escaped. They had locked down the perimeter before they entered the building. It was only dumb luck that she had managed to get off a shot and slip past the agent stationed out back. The bullet had entered and exited the man's shoulder, but Dixon had been informed that he would be all right. The helicopter already had him en route to the nearest hospital.

"I assume he's with Cabot," Dixon continued. "I think I can figure out where they are. What I want to know is, what are they planning?"

"Well, we're all here visiting this fine city of yours," Susan said. "I suspect they're just taking in the sites. Lots of places to see. Tar pits. Hollywood sign. Don't forget the maps to the stars' homes."

Dixon and the woman continued to go round and round with the questioning for about five minutes before he gave up. He wasn't going to get anything out of her here. And he wasn't about to torture her either. The last thing he wanted to do was be the one to prove what she thought about American intelligence agents was right.

He considered waking one of the other operatives but decided against it. They would probably be just as unwilling to give Dixon what he wanted, and he wasn't in the position to offer any deals. Besides, he hadn't been lying when he told the woman he suspected where Cabot and Reed had gone. It was fairly obvious once the two had been unaccounted for.

Dixon left the conference room where they had gathered the Thirteen Stars operatives. Once he was out of earshot, he turned on his comm and linked with APO headquarters and Sydney's team.

"This is Outrigger," he reported. "We've got eight of the operatives. Cabot and the tech guy, Reed, are missing. No one here's talking yet, but I think we can guess where they've gone."

CHAPTER 19

DOWNTOWN LOS ANGELES

"They want Sloane," Sydney said to Weiss beside her. She was sure the entire team had come to the same conclusion but didn't want to mention him by name over the comm. It made perfect sense. She had somehow reawakened Cabot's obsession with Arvin Sloane. And now he was going to get the revenge he had been waiting to exact for about fifteen years.

"Our guys won't talk either. Or, more specifically, they won't talk about the things we want them to talk about," Vaughn said as he came out of the building where the two operatives had been caught and were still being held. He removed his mask. "They won't shut up about things we have no interest in. But they did confirm that Reed was with Cabot. I don't think they *realized* that they confirmed it, but they confirmed it."

"Raptor, can you make contact?" Sydney asked into her comm. "Warn the target that Cabot's gunning for him."

"I just tried his phone, but he didn't respond," Jack replied. "His speech must have started. I'm contacting Evergreen and patching her in."

Sydney yanked off her blond wig. "Let's go," she said to Vaughn as she moved for the car. "We've got to get to the convention center."

"What about Tweedledum and Tweedledumber?" Weiss asked.

"See what you can get out of them," Vaughn replied as he threw his mask to his friend.

"Will do!" Weiss's lips curled into an evil smile as he took off his overcoat and threw on Vaughn's black mask to hide his identity. "Call *me* pudgy."

Sydney hopped behind the wheel and started up the car. Vaughn had barely gotten the passenger-side door closed before she took off, kicking up gravel behind her.

"I can't believe we're saving Sloane's life again," Sydney said as she tried to control her anger. "It's bad enough we have to work with him."

"At least you get to be there for his speech," Vaughn said, trying to add a little levity to the situation. It didn't work.

"I've got Evergreen," Jack said as he came back over the comm.

"The speech just started," Nadia whispered as she was patched in. Sydney could hear Sloane's voice droning on in the background, but she couldn't make out what he was saying. "I don't see Cabot, but the room is dark right now. I'm pulling the target off the dais."

"No. Wait," Sydney said. Her mind was racing as quickly as she was driving through the train yards. Since security had previously cleared the area for them, it was much easier to get around not having to worry about hitting innocent people. Instead she could focus on the question nagging at her. There had to be a reason the tech guy went along on the mission. "What's scheduled for after his speech?"

"Hold on," Nadia said. Sydney could hear Nadia whispering to someone. "The PA says there's some kind of multimedia presentation."

"That's it!" Sydney said. "Find out where the broadcast room is. You need to stop the presentation."

"Okay," Nadia said. "But first I'm getting the target off the stage."

"No," Sydney said as she tore out of the train yards and onto the streets of Los Angeles. She needed to pay slightly more attention to the driving now that there were civilians in the way. "Do that and Cabot will get away. Trust me. He's not going to do anything until after the presentation."

"How do you know that?" Jack asked from headquarters.

"Why did Cabot need to hack into those particular files?" Sydney asked rhetorically. "There wasn't much in there that he didn't know. But that wasn't the point. He needed the official files so he could use them. Cabot doesn't just want to kill the target, he wants to destroy him."

"How so?" Vaughn asked as he held on tightly while Sydney whipped the car around a corner.

"I think he's switched the original presentation with the files," Sydney said. "He plans to put the target on trial in front of the world, then execute him for his crimes."

"And put the Agency on trial by default," Jack added, referring to the CIA. "For letting a criminal get away with everything in the files."

And for continuing to work with that criminal, Sydney thought.

"That's insane," Vaughn said.

"Evergreen, you need to stop the presentation," Sydney said.

There was a long pause as Nadia weighed her options.

"Listen to me," Sydney said, "we started something here that we didn't intend to. Cabot isn't going to let this rest. It's like he keeps getting slapped down for something where he was right all along. If he gets away, he's going to keep on coming back. We have to end this now."

"I'm on my way to the broadcast room," Nadia said as she hung up her phone.

"I know I don't need to tell you how bad this will be if Cabot succeeds with the presentation," Jack said, leaving out any reference to the possible assassination of Sloane. "And not solely for the target. The man needs to be stopped."

"I know," Sydney said as she swung the car left to avoid traffic congestion. The convention center was only three miles away, but it was rush hour downtown. That meant side streets and creative driving for the next few minutes if Sydney wanted to get there in time.

"Let's hope that Sloane is a long-winded speaker," Vaughn said.

"I wouldn't be surprised," she said.

Sydney twisted and turned the car through the downtown streets. She went the wrong way a couple times and hopped a curb or two, but managed to get to the convention center in under seven minutes. She pulled up at the front of the center and came to a screeching halt in a reserved spot marked, fittingly, FOR AUTHORIZED PERSONNEL ONLY.

"The presentation is in the West Hall," Sydney said as they raced into the building. "Hall B."

Sydney had been inside the convention center only a couple times in her life. She wasn't sure where she was going, but there were conveniently placed signs pointing her and Vaughn in the right direction. They ran along the glass and metal concourse to the West Hall lobby. With its white beams and polished floors it reminded Sydney a bit of APO headquarters.

Sydney pulled out her cell phone and tried to call Nadia. She went directly to voice mail but didn't bother leaving a message. Sydney hoped that wasn't a bad sign.

As they reached the West Hall lobby, Sydney saw an information booth where an older woman in a blazer sat ready to provide directions. She hoped the woman would have the answer she was looking for.

"Where is the broadcast room for hall B?" she asked the attendant without bothering with pleasantries.

"Why, hello," the woman said, happy to assist as she scrolled down her listing of occupied spaces. "I believe . . . Yes. They've set up in the gallery directly across from the hall entrance," the woman said, pointing Sydney in the direction of the broadcast booth.

"You go secure Sloane," Sydney said to Vaughn. "I'll make sure Nadia stopped the presentation."

Vaughn headed for the hall while Sydney continued to the left toward the gallery, as the woman had indicated. If Nadia had done her job, then Sydney had nothing to worry about. In the seven minutes it took to get to the convention center, Nadia could easily have stopped the presentation and calmly pulled Sloane off the stage before Cabot even noticed.

But why didn't she answer her phone? Sydney wondered, naturally assuming that everything hadn't gone as planned.

The door to the broadcast room was open a crack, but Sydney couldn't see anything inside. She took stock of the situation. The odds were that Nadia had already gone in, secured the area, and taken care of the potentially damning presentation. Sydney would have preferred to have confirmed that with the phone call. Not knowing what she would find inside the room, Sydney reached into her jacket to grab her gun as she pushed the door open and entered the room.

The gallery was set up with rows of monitors and equipment for the proceedings to be broadcast to the "global Omnifam family." Sydney saw Sloane up on the monitors. He was talking about the successful work in building new water-treatment facilities in third-world countries. But Sydney had no interest in hearing what he had to say. Something else had stolen her attention.

Five technicians were sitting in front of the first bank of monitors. Each one had his or her head down on the table in front of them. They were out cold. Sydney could tell from the rise and fall of their backs that they were asleep. That didn't surprise her. Cabot wasn't interested in harming innocent victims.

For a brief moment Sydney considered allowing the presentation to go forward. She wasn't sure exactly what was in Sloane's file, but she figured that she could guess most of the contents. Especially considering she and her father were probably the ones who'd provided most of the information.

It was tempting. It would certainly take care of her largest issue with working for APO. But it was also another one of those fine lines she knew she couldn't cross. This was not the way it was supposed to work. There were rules to this kind of thing. If she just went along with Cabot's plans, she would be turning her back on everything she had worked for over the years. She would be giving up on the one person she trusted to know when to do the right thing: herself.

Sydney pulled her gun. She heard shuffling from behind the first row of monitors. Considering that the technicians were all asleep, it was likely that Reed or Cabot was in the room. The wall of equipment was impossible to see through and too tall to see over. It sounded like someone was tampering with the system, though. That much Sydney could tell.

She quietly entered the room and moved past the table of sleeping technicians. She stopped when she came to the end of the row. It was possible that it was just Nadia back there setting everything right after having dealt with Cabot and Reed. However, Sydney didn't think that was the case. Since she couldn't tell what direction the person was facing on the other side of the monitors, Sydney knew she had to go in fast and with her gun drawn.

Sydney turned the corner and saw the back of an unfamiliar man. He was fiddling with the equipment. She wasn't exactly sure what he was doing, but she could probably figure it out. The one thing she did know for certain was that it was not Harrison Cabot.

"Step away from the equipment, Mr. Reed," Sydney said.

"Actually, Reed's the first name," he replied as he stopped what he was doing, put his hands up, and turned to her. "And it's too late, Ms. Bristow. The presentation is going to begin in a minute, whether or not Sloane ever shuts up."

There was an image frozen on the two monitors behind him. The words on the screen read, "The Truth about Arvin Sloane." She could still hear Sloane making his speech over the other monitors. It seemed like he was starting to wrap things up.

"I've locked in the DVD," Reed said. "You can't stop it. No one can stop it."

Sydney doubted he was telling the truth. This was a simple broadcast booth, not some high-tech company's computer mainframe. In all likelihood it was simply a matter of flipping a switch somewhere. Too bad she didn't know where to begin.

She stepped up to the jumble of equipment, keeping one eye, and her gun, trained on Reed the entire time. Sydney had absorbed a fair amount of knowledge about computer systems over the years, but this hodgepodge of roughly cabled together technology left her at a loss. She couldn't imagine that this was a standard setup.

Sydney quickly considered her options.

Pulling the fire alarm was certainly an easy out. The event organizers would have to bring up the lights in the hall, making it almost impossible to see the video screen while everyone filed out of the room. But that didn't take care of the image being broadcast around the world via satellite. Time was ticking down and Sydney had to come up with a way to stop the broadcast. Then she realized something she had forgotten.

Reed thought she was one of the bad guys.

Sydney turned to the technician and smiled. She raised her gun and held it to his forehead. "Stop the broadcast," she said coldly. "Now."

"I can't do that," Reed said. "Arvin Sloane has to be stopped."

Sydney watched as a drop of sweat rolled down his forehead. She felt bad for the kid. He reminded her a bit of Mini-Marshall. They were both around the same age and obviously technical geniuses. But this guy was working on the wrong side of the law. As much as she respected him for sticking to his convictions, she had to stop him before he did something the law would consider problematic.

She cocked her gun. "Stop. The. Broadcast."

Reed was trembling, which didn't make Sydney

feel any better. But she had assumed her alias. She was the terrorist Reed believed her to be. She was a killer.

She looked him stone-cold in the eye and removed any doubt that he was about to die.

"Okay!" he said quickly. "I'll stop it. I swear."

"Go ahead," she said, keeping the gun to his forehead.

Reed carefully stepped past her to the wall of technology. He pressed a series of buttons and the DVD ejected from a slot a few feet away. The two monitors went blank.

"Is that it?" Sydney asked.

"That's it," he said, resigned.

At that same moment, Sloane wrapped up his speech to thunderous applause. It was bad enough that she had to listen to the adulation over the sound system, but she could hear the cheers live and in person from across the hall. There was a large segment of society that absolutely loved Sloane.

The thought sickened Sydney.

She removed the gun from Reed's forehead and reset the hammer. "I'm sorry about this," she said, before slamming the butt of the gun into his head and knocking him unconscious.

Sydney used a zip tie to bind Reed to a metal bar that ran along the wall of monitors. She left the broadcast booth and went across the way to the West Hall entrance. People were still standing and applauding. In all the commotion it was hard to see Sloane and Vaughn.

Sloane had wrapped up his presentation, and everyone was settling back into their seats to wait for the video to start. Sydney imagined the same thing was happening at Omnifam events around the world. *Sorry to disappoint you guys*, Sydney thought, *but there's not going to be a show today.*

Once everyone was seated, the lights went down for the video. Before it went dark, Sydney could see that Vaughn was standing at the side of the dais with Sloane. Sydney joined them as Vaughn finished filling their boss in on what had nearly happened.

"Thank you, Sydney," Sloane said as she came up to him. "I owe my—"

"Save it," Sydney said. "Where's Nadia?"

"Cabot didn't want me," Sloane said in shock as the reality of the situation set in. "He wants me to *suffer* like he did. I took his partner. He's taking my daughter."

"But how—," Sydney started to say.

"There was a photo and information on her in my file," Sloane said. "I put her on the guest list for this event under her own name. If Thirteen Stars could hack into Martine's computer, getting into the Omnifam corporate guest list would be nothing. They were after Nadia."

Sydney had only seen Sloane look this way once before. It was following the supposed death of his wife, Emily. The first death, that is. But that emotion had been faked, much like her death. This was real.

"Mr. Sloane." A young production assistant–type came up to the group, interrupting. "We're so sorry. There seems to be something wrong with the video. And the tech crew, come to think of it. Just wanted to let you know—"

"Go away," Sloane said to the poor guy, who didn't know what he was getting in the middle of. "Now!"

Sydney couldn't blame Sloane for reacting the way that he was, but she needed to get control of the situation if she was going to save Nadia. If it wasn't already too late.

"Okay," Sydney said, trying to wrap her head around the situation. Nadia was her family too. She had just found her sister. She wasn't about to lose her now. "Cabot wouldn't just take off with her. He'd want you to see. He'd want you to know what happened."

"Would he be sick enough to re-create what happened to his partner?" Vaughn asked. "Would he take her somewhere in the city? Somewhere that only you would know about."

"No," Sloane replied. "It didn't happen that way."

Sydney didn't want to ask the question but knew she had to if she was going to find Nadia. She braced herself for another horrific admission of a past guilt. "What did you do?"

"It wasn't me," Sloane said, drawing out his words. "It was the Alliance. They ordered me. I ordered someone else."

"Who?" Sydney asked, praying that he wasn't about to say her father.

"Doesn't matter," Sloane said numbly. "He's gone now. I think Cabot managed to take him out a couple years ago. I'm the only one left in this equation."

"We need you to focus," Sydney said. "We're running out of time. Cabot is going to kill your daughter."

That snapped Sloane out of his daze. "My car," he said. "Cabot had to be warned off. He was just starting to investigate SD-6. We sent him a message. His partner was . . . left for him. In his car." It was as if Sloane had just woken up and realized that he wasn't alone. "Sydney, you have to stop him. I'm parked on the second level of the structure."

"We're on our way," Sydney said.

"I'll be right behind you," Sloane said.

"No!" Sydney wheeled on him. The last thing she needed was Sloane in the mix. "You stay right here."

"Sydney, she's my *daughter*," he insisted.

"Which is why I don't want you anywhere near this," Sydney replied. "Now stop wasting my time."

"Go," Sloane said.

Sydney didn't wait a moment longer, and she and Vaughn took off. She was still concerned that Sloane would follow and complicate the situation, but she couldn't waste her time worrying about that. Her focus needed to be on Nadia.

As she and Vaughn raced out of the hall heading for the West Hall parking structure, she remembered that Reed was still in the broadcast booth bound to the equipment. If the event organizers were in there trying to figure out what had gone wrong with the video equipment, it was possible they would accidentally let him go. APO couldn't risk letting any of the operatives of Thirteen Stars get away. Especially one who had seen Sydney while she was supposedly in federal custody.

"Reed!" Sydney said without stopping. "He's in the broadcast booth."

"I'll take care of him," Vaughn said. "You go after Nadia."

Sydney didn't even slow to thank him. She continued down the hallway and slammed out the doors to the parking structure. Taking the steps two at a time, she flew up to the second floor. Her gun was out. She wasn't concerned about running into any civilians. Everyone was still inside waiting for the multimedia presentation that would probably never come.

The second floor of the parking structure seemed empty of people, but Sydney knew Cabot was there with Nadia. He had to be.

She started off to her left, looking for Sloane's car. Row after row of SUVs made the search difficult and dangerous. Cabot could have been holding Nadia behind any of the tall vehicles. One by one Sydney worked her way past the vehicles.

Sydney continued up the ramp and around the corner. As she was nearing what would be considered the third level, she began to fear that she had chosen the wrong direction. But that was when she saw them.

Cabot had his back to her, but Nadia saw that she was no longer alone. They were standing at Sloane's car. From Sydney's vantage point, she couldn't tell what Cabot was trying to do.

Sydney slowly approached the car while her sister distracted Cabot. As she got closer, Sydney could see that Cabot was working on breaking into the car in what Marshall would call the "old-school style." He had slipped a metal slat between the passenger door and window. The lock was popped open within seconds.

Sydney knew she could play this several ways. Considering she was about to lose the element of surprise, she chose to go with the direct route.

"Hello, Mr. Cabot," she said from a secured position behind the car.

He turned toward her with a smile masking his surprise. "Please . . . call me Harry."

"I don't think I will," Sydney said, remembering back to the meet that had started this all, when Sprague had asked her to call him Maxie. She hadn't intended to get familiar with that enemy. She certainly wasn't going to buddy up with this one.

"I kind of figured you'd show up," Cabot said. "I didn't believe it when Susan told me that the Feds had you in custody. Haven't quite figured out your game plan yet, but we will."

Sydney could tell that Cabot didn't know he was the only member of Thirteen Stars not in custody. He was still referring to his team as "we." Sadly, now it was just an organization of one man.

She was glad that he wasn't quite in the loop. It would help her negotiate the situation so that it played out according to *her* terms.

"Let her go," Sydney said, emphasizing the demand with her gun.

"I don't think so," Cabot replied. He shifted his body to reveal his own gun pointed at Nadia's gut. "See, I've got one too."

"She didn't do anything to you," Sydney said.

"Do you know who this is?" Cabot asked, which told Sydney that Sloane's file apparently wasn't totally complete. Cabot didn't know about the link between Sydney and Nadia. "Of course you do. You're working for her father. See. I was right about that, wasn't I? That's why you're here now."

"How about we make a deal?" Sydney asked.

"You *still* don't understand what I'm about, do

you?" Cabot asked. "You haven't quite grasped the mission of Thirteen Stars."

"Why don't you spell it out for me," Sydney suggested, to keep him talking and keep his mind off Nadia.

"I don't make deals with criminals," he said.

"I'll destroy the core," Sydney offered, playing into her character again. "If you let her go. Sloane would rather have his daughter than some weapon."

"Somehow I doubt that," Cabot said.

Sydney didn't, though. It was the one thing she accepted about Sloane without question. The *only* thing.

"I have a better idea," Cabot said. "Give me the core and I'll let her go."

"You're insane if you think I'm letting you have that weapon," Sydney said. "I trust you with it about as much as you trust me."

"I'll kill her," he replied, jabbing the gun farther into Nadia's side.

Through it all Nadia remained silent. She just looked into Sydney's eyes, silently telling Sydney that Nadia didn't consider her life more important than the danger of letting a man like this obtain the seismic bomb. But just as Sydney wasn't about to *trade* her sister's life for some technology, she wasn't going to *risk* her life for it either.

"You expect me to trade one life for a bomb that could kill millions? I'm not about to do that." Sydney wasn't about to tell him the casing had been destroyed or that there was no instruction disc and the core was now basically useless. She would lose her bargaining power. "It's safer if no one has the whole bomb."

"You really think that Arvin Sloane is going to rest until he has the complete device?" Cabot asked. "I won't let that happen. Once I have the device, I will dismantle it and destroy the files. Trust me."

"Trust you? You're holding an innocent woman at gunpoint to get back at an old enemy," Sydney pointed out. "What happens when you get mad at some foreign government and think they need to be taught a lesson? Do you change your mind about using the bomb? Where do you draw the line?"

"Don't worry about me. I know how to tell the difference."

"Do you? Do you really?" Sydney asked, realizing what she had been missing all along. "Then why didn't you destroy the bomb casing already?"

"I needed to make sure it didn't fall into the wrong hands," Cabot said weakly.

"Tearing the thing apart would have pretty much done that," Sydney said. "But you didn't. Because part of you wanted to hold on to it. Because you knew how valuable it could be."

"That's ridiculous," Cabot insisted. He was getting more agitated. Sydney was worried about upsetting him too much, but she knew that would be Nadia's only chance to get away. She had to risk it.

"Is it?" Sydney asked. "What has this woman done to you? What does *Nadia* have to do with your vendetta against Sloane? You're about to kill an innocent person to prove what? You're not serving the greater good by her death."

"You should talk about serving the greater good," Cabot replied, swinging the gun in her direction to emphasize his point.

"Yes," Sydney said. "I should. Because, you know the difference between you and me? At the end of the day, I still know who I am. I *know* what side I'm on. Can you say the same?"

"Don't—"

Nadia cut off Cabot's comment by sending a hard elbow into his side, catching him totally by surprise.

She followed the blow with a fist to the face.

Dazed, Cabot dropped the gun. Nadia scooped it up and stepped away from him, backing up toward her sister but keeping Cabot in sight.

"You okay, sis?" Sydney asked.

"Fine, sis," Nadia replied.

Sydney enjoyed the look of shock on Cabot's face. "Guess you don't know everything," she said.

Nadia covered Cabot as Sydney took a zip tie out of her pocket and bound Cabot's hands behind his back. As she did this, Sydney scanned the area, expecting to see Sloane arrive to kill Cabot. But he wasn't there.

Once Cabot's hands were bound, Sydney led him out of the parking structure with Nadia bringing up the rear. They were heading back to the West Hall where Sydney assumed APO members dressed as FBI agents were waiting. Not everyone could have managed her rush-hour drive from Union Station to the convention center in under seven minutes.

Sydney no longer questioned the logic behind taking the Thirteen Stars operatives into custody. There were too many variables in the vigilante business. If Cabot proved anything it was that *some* people who were motivated to take justice into their own hands couldn't be trusted to not blur the lines between their responsibility to themselves and their responsibility to the world.

Once again Sydney had to accept there was no such thing as clear-cut good and evil. Cabot's own mission had been overwhelmed by his desire for revenge. It was the opposite of how Sydney approached her life. She used her need for revenge against Sloane to motivate her to continue working for the side of good. And that was how she justified the smaller evils—the Spragues and Martines and everyone else she was forced into dealing with. Because at the end of the day, she knew she was doing more good than evil.

And maybe that was all that she needed to know.

"So I managed to catch some of Sloane's speech," Sydney said to her sister as they walked back into the building.

"Really?" Nadia replied lightly. "I missed it entirely. How was it?"

"A little dry," Sydney said. "But I hear the video presentation is something worth seeing."

Paul Ruditis is the author of *Authorized Personnel Only*, the official guide to the first four seasons of *Alias*. He has also written and contributed to numerous books based on such popular series as *Buffy the Vampire Slayer*, *Angel*, *Charmed*, *Star Trek*, *Queer as Folk*, and *The West Wing*.

He lives in Burbank, California.